Nim·bo·stra·tus

ˌnimbōˈstradəs,ˌnimbōˈstrādəs/

noun

noun: **nimbostratus**

a cloud of a class characterized by a formless layer that is almost uniformly dark gray; a rain cloud of the layer type, of low altitude, usually below 8000 feet (2440 meters).

NIMBOSTRATUS

Rain Clouds of Death

HANK PATTERSON

To order additional copies of this book, contact:
Xlibris
1-888-795-4274
www.Xlibris.com
Orders@Xlibris.com
767435

This book is dedicated in loving memory to my grandmother. Thelma Warfield, grandfather Clarence Warfield and my father Henry Patterson. May you all continue to soar with the angels!

CHAPTER 1

"It looks like another beautiful day here in Aruba. The weather forecast is currently 80 degrees Fahrenheit, partly cloudy/windy, with scattered showers this morning that will become a steady light rain during the afternoon hours. High 88 degrees Fahrenheit. Winds from the east are at 15–25 miles per hour. Tonight, it's windy, with scattered showers this evening, becoming—"

"Najee, come on, you're going to make us late," a voice called from outside.

"more widespread overnight. It's going to be a low 79 degrees Fahrenheit, with winds from the east at 15 to 25 miles per hour. Chance of rain is at 60 percent. I'm Tim Coles, and I'll be right back with the rest of the week's forecast."

"Coming," a deep voice called back as he shut off the TV. "Hey, Sheila, did you grab the portable?"

"Yes, dear, now come on, we want to get to the dock before our guests arrive. I'll drive." Sheila hopped in the driver's seat of the Dodge pickup. Najee got in, and she took off down the road. "So what did they say about the weather?"

"Sixty percent chance of rain. We'll take them to the eastern side of the island and catch a few rain clouds there."

Sheila was a short white woman who had moved to the island about two years ago from Holland. Najee was a native of the island and spoke all four of its languages. It was six fifteen on a Sunday morning, and they had booked a tourist group of six to go deep-sea fishing on the boat they owned and had named the *Two of Us*.

"Great," Sheila said as they pulled up to the dock. "Let's get this stuff unloaded before anyone arrives."

"Sure, honey."

Just as they finished unloading, a van pulled up. Three men and three women hopped out. They were all young, in their late twenties. None were married, just couples vacationing, one of the men named Jeff told Najee yesterday when they booked the trip.

"They're here, Sheila," Najee said. "Good morning, everyone. My name is Najee. I'm your captain, and Sheila here is my first mate and your hostess for today."

Jeff introduced the rest of his gang, "This is Bobby, Pam, Susan, Rob, Alicia, and I'm Jeff."

"Well, let's get you all and your gear on board and head out. It's going to be a beautiful day for marlin, barracuda, and yellow tuna fishing today."

CHAPTER 2

It was Sunday, February 14, 2003, 5:00 a.m. Louis woke up sweating and appeared to be shaken by the gruesome dream he'd just had. He sat up for a moment and listened to the rain. Then he got up, peered out the window, and put the TV on. It was cloudy; rain was coming down steady. He hoped it wouldn't affect their flight. Today, they were going to get away from all this godforsaken miserable weather.

Louis Alexander, a black man of forty-three, and his immediate family had been planning this vacation for about a year and a half now. His wife Trish, age thirty-seven, his daughter Lazarr, and his son Lou Jr. were all excited about their upcoming vacation. It had been three years since they had gone anywhere, and the kids were not kids anymore. They were both in their teens—Lazarr, nineteen, and Lou Jr., thirteen.

The other members of the family included Big G and Little G, short for George and George. Big George was hanging out with the family as always. He was, in fact, part of the family. Little George had his own family now. He had a beautiful wife whom they called Sugar, and his daughter Brie. Louis and Little George were brothers. Although they were not the closest of brothers because of the eleven-year age gap, they were tight as any brothers could be. Their mother was Lethia Warfield. Everyone was going to meet up at Lethia's house and catch a shuttle to the airport. The flight was leaving at 8:00 a.m.

CHAPTER 3

"Now boarding rows ten and up," the flight attendant announced.

"That's us," Louis said as he and the rest of his family got up. They made their way onto the plane, and Louis noticed the flight was full. His family was in rows two and three. It was one of those big charter planes with seats in the middle and on both sides. Louis took the window seat, his wife took the aisle seat, and Lou Jr. took the middle. The rest of the family positioned themselves in center rows. Then it came over him, a cold chill going down his spine. He felt uneasy and suddenly very scared. His wife must have noticed, as she leaned over and asked, "You all right, honey?"

"Yeah, I'm fine." He was lying. It was something about the dream he'd had that made him feel this way. He decided he would get a couple of drinks as soon as the flight was under way.

"Welcome to Sunjet Vacations," the stewardess was saying. "Please look at the monitors above you." She stuck a video in. The tape showed the safety functions and escape exits in case of an emergency. They were finally moving. The jet sped down the runway, and they were in the air.

"Good morning," a voice came over the speaker. "My name is Stan. I'm your pilot this morning, and my good friend Roger is my copilot for this trip. Welcome aboard Flight 1155, nonstop to Aruba. We'll be traveling at 500 miles per hour at thirty thousand feet. Flying time is five hours fifteen minutes. The current temperature in Aruba is 80 degrees with scattered showers, at landing it should be clear and around 88 degrees. Please feel free to move around the cabin when the 'fasten seat belt' sign is turned off, and thank you for flying Sunjet Vacations on TTA Airlines."

* * *

Najee had been en route for close to three hours when he came under the rain cloud and dropped anchor. "Here we are, ladies and gentlemen."

Sheila was cleaning up the food and drink that was served while they were on their way. A nice reggae CD was playing. "Fucking yes, this is it, boys. It's time to separate the men from the pussies."

"Well, Jeff, then I guess you better hope Alicia eats you tonight because the fish belong to me today," Rob said as he raised his hand and gave Bobby a high five. "And just to make it a little more competitive, I'll wager you boys $100 for the biggest catch of the day."

"We're in," Bobby and Jeff both replied.

"Grab the bait and the beer and strap us into our chairs, Mr. Najee, and let's rock and roll," Jeff said. Pam and Susan had already made it to the front of the boat and were applying suntan lotion on themselves.

"Are you going to join us, Alicia?" Pam asked as she removed her top and sunned her breasts.

"Maybe later. I'm going to go scuba diving and check out the coral reef and the shipwreck Najee told us about." Alicia was a very experienced diver. She put on her gear, told everyone she'd see them in an hour, and jumped in the clear blue Caribbean Sea. Pam and Susan, now both topless, lay on some of the lounge chairs in the front part of the boat. They were talking about how they were going to get eaten out and laid by their boyfriends tonight. Jeff, Bobby, and Rob were in the back of the boat getting stoned and drunk, talking about all the hot chicks on the island and how they should sneak out and get some island girls later in the week.

Najee came over the loudspeaker. "OK, everyone appears to be settled in. Sheila and I will be below. You know where everything is, so just knock if anyone needs anything, and enjoy your day on the *Two of Us*." He grabbed a bottle of rum, grabbed Sheila's ass, and headed down.

When he looked up at the sky, he saw that the total look of the cloud had seemed to change. It appeared to be lower than before. Darker. It even gave the appearance of some monstrous beast from hell. "That's strange. I've never seen a cloud look like that before"

"Oh come on, baby." Sheila grabbed his dick. "Mommy's hot." The two went below, entered the room, and shut the door. Najee turned the music up so no one would hear them fucking, screaming, and pounding the bed because they always made loud love.

Alicia had descended about thirty feet. She swam around the coral reef, admiring its beauty. She wished her twin sister Sandra was with her, but she'd been unable to get off work from NASA because of the shuttle accident. At any rate, it was peaceful, all the different tropical fishes swimming freely around her as she neared the shipwreck.

Above, the sky started to rumble. "Here we go, boys," Jeff said. You could smell the rain, which meant the larger fish would surface to the top for even smaller fish and insects.

The music was blaring, and the sky was rumbling. Down below, Sheila was screaming, "Fuck me! Fuck me! Ahh yes! Fuck me harder!"

Najee slapped her ass. "You like it, baby?"

"Oh yes, give it to me harder, fuck me in my ass!" Najee and Sheila didn't hear the horrifying screams from above. They were so in tune with each other.

It started to trickle a few raindrops. Pam screamed as the first raindrop hit her body. "What is it?" Susan sat up and asked.

She screamed again, this time looking down at her leg and arm. They were burning—the rain was burning her. It felt like her skin was melting off where the few drops had hit her. The sky rumbled, and slow, steady rain came upon them.

Jeff was the first of the men to scream. He dropped his line and grabbed his head. He was screaming, but he couldn't get out of his seat. The rain was burning through his skull; blood was running down his head as it started to deteriorate.

Now they were all screaming as the rain started to pour down hard. Pam's eyeballs were melting away from the raindrops that had gotten into them. It was like some someone had poured some industrial agents containing alkalis in them. As the rain hit her body, it burned right though her skin and burned her heart out, along with the rest of her organs. Right before she died, she felt as if she was being lowered into an acid bath that melted your skin off until you were nothing but a skeleton. Susan had gotten up and started to run as the rain-like acid ate away at her. She was bloody and had almost made it out of the rain when the rain puddles on the deck ate her feet, and she fell and withered away into nothingness.

Najee and Sheila were dripping sweat now, as if they were in a steam room. He was licking the sweat off her back as he continued to pound into her ass. She continued to scream and holler, "Give me more! Give me all the dick you have!"

In the back of the boat sat three skeletons still strapped to their chairs. The rain had burned them from head to toe. The rain stopped. Blood and bones covered the deck, some blood dripping down the side of the boat and into the sea.

Najee pulled his dick out of Sheila's ass and gave out a loud howl as he shot cum all over her back. He rubbed the cum on her back as if he were putting lotion on her, turned her around, gripped her breast hard, and kissed her. The two of them lay down and smiled at each other.

"You think they caught anything?" Sheila asked as she turned the music down.

Jeff's bell began to ring. "He had a catch."

"Sounds like it, let's go see."

CHAPTER 4

Sandra Blake was a radiation specialist for NASA, her specialty being nuclear radiation and radioactive particles. She sat alone, drinking a cup of coffee in the cafeteria at work this morning, thinking of her sister Alicia. Sandra was worried. When you had an identical twin, you could sense when the other was in trouble, no matter how far away they were. This morning, the feeling was unbearable. She had to get her boss to give her some time off. She would tell him it was a family emergency. She had tried to reach Alicia early this morning but to no avail. Sandra finished her coffee, got up, went to her office, and checked for flight availability to Aruba.

Sandra made her home in New Mexico and worked at the White Sands Test Facility in Las Cruces. She was on loan to the Kennedy Space Center in Florida, not far from Miami. She would drive down and catch a flight from there. There were plenty of flights leaving, so she could leave today. Sandra picked up her phone and called her boss, explaining to him the nature of the urgency. She was given permission to leave. She would run by her rented condo, pack some stuff, drive to Miami, and be on the 3:00 p.m. flight.

CHAPTER 5

Louis was awake again. He'd gotten some sleep, but he had dreamed again—not the same dream of screaming, but something about clouds. Or was it just that they were flying through the clouds? At any rate, they were about an hour away from landing. It was time to use the toilet and stretch his legs. He looked out the window at the clouds and shivered. *Why is this happening to me?* he asked himself as he made his way to the toilet.

He could see his brother getting up, which was cool. He would chat with him for a while. George walked up to him and said, "Man, I was knocked out, but I had some fucked-up dream while I was sleep."

"Yeah? About what?"

"Some bullshit about clouds I can't even remember."

"No shit, George. I dreamed some stupid shit like that too. I figured it was just because we're flying through them, but that's some weird shit for us to both be dreaming or be thinking about the same shit. Especially since it ain't any bitches."

George laughed. "What bitches are you gon' be thinking about with the whole family here?"

"Hey, I can still look, can't I? You know how it be layin' out here."

"Yeah, you're right."

Louis stepped in the lavatory, did his thing, and headed back for his seat, thinking of how strange it was for his brother to mention clouds.

* * *

Alicia looked at how much time she had left and started back for the boat. She was very relaxed now and excited to be here in Aruba with her friends. She wondered if they had caught anything. At any rate, she was ready to take in some sun and have one of those nice island drinks Sheila had been whipping up all morning.

Najee and Sheila came out from below, and at first, all they saw was blood. "What the shit," Najee said. And then Sheila screamed. Najee began to vomit as he saw bones, bits of organs, and flesh strewn across the deck. He was leaning over the side of the rails when he heard the thunder, but he was too sick, too frightened to move.

"What the hell had happened and how? Who could have done something like this?" Sheila was on her knees crying. Najee knew they had to get a distress signal out. With all the bones everywhere, he couldn't be sure if Alicia had made it back. Did she do this? He had to calm himself. He picked Sheila up off the deck and headed to the top of the boat, where he kept his gun and where he could make the distress call.

"Najee," she said, crying, "we have to get out of here."

"I know." The clouds were almost pitch black over the boat. He sat Sheila down and made the distress call. Then it started, the burning rain. Sheila had been mutilated pretty badly by the time she jumped overboard, but it was too late for her. She drowned. Najee had made it to some shelter on the boat where the rain couldn't get him, but he too was badly mutilated. Again, the rain stopped.

"You bastards!" Alicia was screaming as she climbed up the ladder. "Somebody give me a fucking hand!" She reached the top and saw the skeletons of the three men. She started screaming, letting go of the ladder. She could feel herself falling backward when a bloody hand reached out and grabbed her.

The half-mutilated figure looked like something out of a horror movie, and she struggled to free herself from its grasp. Najee didn't let go of her, pulling her on board and dragging her to the cabin below. She was kicking and screaming all the way. She couldn't understand what was happening. She saw the body parts and organs all over. Najee was pointing to the sky and saying something about the rain. She was too scared to think straight, and at that moment, she dug her fingers into his face and pulled the rest of his already half-mutilated flesh off. She really freaked out once she noticed she had his bloody flesh in her hand and started screaming more.

Najee punched her in the jaw, and she was out cold. He threw her in the room and lay down outside the door so she could not get out.

*   *   *

The distress signal had come into the beach police station, and Lt. Caleb Sipe and Capt. Luis Sanchez were en route to its origin. They couldn't make out what Najee was saying when he called. They were going full speed, yet it would still take them a little over ninety minutes to get there. Both the island choppers were in for maintenance repairs and were unavailable.

"Try to raise them, Caleb. See if we can get some idea of what's going on out there."

"Yes, sir," Caleb tried to raise the *Two of Us*. "Nothing, sir."

CHAPTER 6

"This is Flight 1155 to tower."

"Yes, Flight 1155, we read you."

"We're currently at 20,000 feet and descending, requesting surface radar and visual."

"Yes, Flight 1155, we have you on radar. Slow your speed to 200 miles per hour, continue your descent at 100 feet per minute, and stand by for current weather conditions."

The air traffic controller checked with Tim Coles, who worked with the airport as well as the news station in Aruba. The news station was about a mile from the airport, so he was linked to their weather radar system as well as the Doppler system for the whole island and the sea lines reaching the neighboring Cuba and Venezuela. Tim was on the phone with the local controller. "Steve, this is Tim. Hey, I'm picking up gusting winds at 45 miles per hour, that's pushing low-level nimbostratus clouds right into the flight path of your plane at 6,500 feet."

"Dammit, Tim, speak English. A what cloud?"

"A dark low-level cloud with precipitation, *full* of water droplets. I think you may have to have them circle the island. If not, tell them to be prepared for some turbulence because of the winds pushing the clouds."

"Too late for the circle. I'll tell them. Thanks, Tim," he said, and then he got back to the pilot. "This is tower to Flight 1155."

"This is Flight 1155, we read you."

"Captain, you have a low-level cloud coming right in your path with rain and winds up to 45 miles per hour at 6,500 feet. Proceed with caution."

"Will do, tower. We'll contact you after we pass through. Please have ground control ready and any paramedics in the area just in case we get a few shaken passengers."

"Copy that, 1155. You're clear to land."

"This is your captain. All passengers, please take your seats. Observe 'fasten your seat belt' signs. Stewards, please check all passengers and prepare for landing. We may run into a little turbulence as we pass through this rain cloud, so please don't be alarmed. Our estimated time of arrival is fifteen minutes. Thank you for flying Sunjet Vacations on TTA Airlines."

This was the part Louis couldn't stand. He looked at his wife and son. They were both asleep. He could hear his mother talking to Big George. Little George was still reading a paper. Sugar was talking to Lazarr and Brie. The plane was full of chatter and people laughing. The stewards made their final checks and were sitting now.

The sky got dark as they descended into the cloud. The plane began to pull to the left, and then right, and then up and down. It was shaking, and the passengers were scared. You could hear raindrops beating on the plane. Louis could swear he heard a sizzling sound, as if something were cooking. He looked out the window. It was dark. He refocused and could swear he saw smoke coming from the plane. Then there was a *loud* boom. The plane jerked left.

In the cockpit, the pilot and copilot were trying their best not to lose control as the plane thrashed up, down, side to side, and all about. "What was that?"

"We just lost engine one, sir," the copilot informed him.

"Call it in, man!" the pilot shouted.

"No good, sir. Can't hold her if I let go."

"Damn!" the pilot shouted.

The passengers were screaming. Some were crying, while most prayed. The plane was actually coming apart. The rain droplets were melting the metal and would soon burn right through. It was getting hot inside the plane. The oxygen masks had fallen, and people were gasping for air.

"Mommy, are we going to crash?" Louis heard a child ask her mother.

"No, baby, we'll be all right. Just hold on to me, and keep the mask on."

There was another loud boom, and Louis looked over at his wife. Her eyes looked as if they were going to pop out of their sockets any second now, and tears were pouring down her face. He grabbed her hand and his son's and began to pray himself.

The shaking stopped, and the sun reappeared. People were thanking God when out of nowhere came another loud boom, but this time, it was accompanied by a squeaking sound. Louis could see the ground. Flight 1155 had landed. The passengers were now cheering and glad to be alive. They wanted off this damn plane. You could see ambulances and fire trucks pulling up. Was there a fire? What had happened during those five minutes of terror? Louis would do his own check later. Right now, it was time to get off the plane.

After getting through customs, Louis and Little George found the driver they had hired and were on their way. The family was staying at Endless Summer, a seven-bedroom villa overlooking the famous Half Moon Golf Course and the Caribbean Sea. Its rooms opened to an 85-foot veranda, where the sweeping 120-degree view of manicured grounds, golf course, and sea and sky was truly breathtaking. Five of the rooms had air-conditioning and were located on the main level—three had ocean views, and two had garden views. Upstairs, via an exterior staircase, were the other bedrooms. The pool shared the deck with a therapeutic spa. The staff included a butler, a cook, a maid, a laundress, and a gardener. Yes, this was going to be a great two weeks.

Once they arrived, the villa was perfect. Louis and his wife Trish, Little George, and Sugar took the upstairs rooms, the rest of the family taking the ones downstairs. They all washed, unpacked, and met under the gazebo for drinks and to talk about the plane ride from hell before dinner. The kids went for a swim.

Louis said, "I don't know if any of you noticed, but it seemed like the plane was burning. No, not burning—like melting, somehow."

"Yes, there was this smell of burnt metal when we got off, and you could see spots of the metal sweltering."

Carl the butler brought their drinks and a deli tray with sandwiches since dinner wouldn't be served until six. He introduced the rest of the staff and told them to just call if there was anything they needed.

Louis held up his glass and said, "Here's a toast to two weeks in paradise and fun in the sun."

His mother added, "And we would just like to say thank you, Lord, for getting us here."

"Amen," the family responded.

CHAPTER 7

Sandra had made the drive to Miami and was in flight. Her flight would take a little over two hours, so she decided to nap on the plane.

The Aruba police had pulled up alongside the *Two of Us* and were boarding the boat. "*My* god," Caleb said. "What happened here?"

"Better call for a tow," Sanchez replied. He pulled out his gun and gagged, trying to hold back the vomit. "You search the top, I'll search below." This time, he couldn't hold it. He leaned over the rail and vomited.

He gathered himself and went down, and then he shouted from below, "I've got one who's only half mutilated but dead!"

He pulled Najee's body from the door and opened it slowly. Alicia was sitting on the floor in the corner with a blank stare.

"Miss, are you all right? We're here to help. Did you make the distress call?"

Alicia didn't answer or move, she just sat there staring and shaking.

"OK, miss, I'm going to get you off this boat and to a hospital."

Caleb entered the room. "Nothing up top, just blood and guts, sir. What do you think happened here?"

"Hard to say, Caleb. Did you call for the tow?"

"Yes, I told them not to come aboard without you, sir. I found these duffel bags. Hopefully, we can ID some of these skeletons."

"Good, let's go. I don't want to spend another second on this boat."

The two men got Alicia on their boat and sped away for shore. "Call the hospital and tell them we have a woman in shock," Sanchez told Caleb. "I don't know what happened out there, but we have a problem."

The doctors admitted Alicia to the trauma ward. She was in pretty bad shape, unresponsive to the entire test and the questions they asked her. They stuck her in a private room and strapped her to her bed so she would not hurt herself. The doctor declined to give her any drugs until they could get some type of medical history on her. Captain Sanchez and Caleb went through the belongings found on the boat and were able to identify Alicia from her license and work ID. Now they had to call the States and try to reach a relative.

"Captain Sanchez, look at this." Caleb showed him a picture of Alicia and Sandra.

"So she has a twin. Great, but where is she?"

Sandra's plane had just landed. As she was walking into the airport, she noticed a lot of mechanics and what seemed to be inspectors of some sort checking out a plane at the end of the hangar. The plane had a lot of outside damage. She wondered what was going on. While she was in the customs line, she overheard some people saying that the plane had almost crashed after something burned right through the metal. She began to worry about Alicia. Sandra got out of customs and took a cab to the resort where Alicia and her friends were staying. She checked with the front desk, but no one was in any of the rooms. Sandra booked a room, had the bellboy take her things up, and decided to get a drink and a burger.

Caleb and Sanchez found out the resort Alicia was in from going through her things and headed over there, hoping to find the number for a relative in her room. They checked with the clerk to get a room key. The clerk pointed to Sandra at the bar. They walked up to Sandra.

"Ms. Blake?" Sanchez asked.

"Yes?"

"I'm Captain Sanchez, this is Lieutenant Caleb." Sanchez pulled out the photo of Alicia. "Sandra, bear with me, please. I have to ask this question. Is this a picture of you and your sister?"

Sandra looked at the picture. "Where did you get this? Where's Alicia? Is she all right?"

"Ms. Blake, we need you to come with us. Alicia was involved in some type of accident."

"I asked if she was all right!"

"She's at the hospital. She hasn't been physically harmed as far as we can tell, but she's in a state of shock."

"What shock? What are you talking about? What happened?"

"Please, Ms. Blake," Sanchez said, "come with us."

Sandra got up and went to the hospital with the officers.

CHAPTER 8

The family had just finished dinner. Louis decided to take a walk down the beach and watch the sunset. Aruba had a beautiful sunset. The way the sun just sank into the water and the cool evening breeze were part of what Louis always came here for. His wife came along for the walk. At first, he was quiet, but he couldn't get the dreams out of his mind, so he decided to share his thoughts with Trish.

"Honey, did I mention the strange dreams I've had last night and on the plane?"

"No, baby. Dreams about what?"

"I can't quite make it out. I know there was lots of screaming and blood. It was as if someone was being tortured, but I can't make it out. Then on the plane, I dreamed about clouds."

"Well, Louis, on the plane, I thought it was over."

"No, before we hit the turbulence. But get this: George said he dreamed about the same thing I did."

"Louis, please, did you and George smoke something before we came for this walk?"

"Forget it. I'm trying to tell you something's strange here on the island this time."

A loud scream stopped them in their tracks. It was the scream of a young woman. Again the scream came, this time more chilling than the first. Louis took off running toward the sound. Trish followed. In the water, he could see half a woman's body. She screamed again. Louis was just about to enter the water when a man emerged from underneath. They started giggling and rolling in the sand.

What the fuck? Louis said to himself. He felt really stupid. Maybe it was the joint that had him tripping now, but that still didn't explain the two dreams.

"You OK, baby?" his wife asked.

"Yeah, just out of breath."

"Here, honey, let's head back to the villa. I've had enough excitement for one day. I think I'll just chill and get in some water sports tomorrow."

CHAPTER 9

Tim Coles was sitting on his deck drinking a beer. His dog lay down next to him panting. He flipped through the pages of some old weather books. There was something about that nimbostratus cloud that grabbed him as being very uncharacteristic for this time of year. His phone rang.

"Hello?"

It was Steve from air traffic control. "Tim, sorry to bother you, but we have a situation back at the airport. I have the pilot of that flight from earlier and the airport's top mechanic here, but we need you to join us."

"What's the problem? I was just getting into this six-pack."

"Tim, I can't say over the phone. We need you now."

"All right, give me twenty minutes," Tim said as he hung up the phone and grabbed his keys and his beer. "See you soon," he called out to his dog who just sat there panting. As he headed for the airport, he knew it had something to do with that nimbostratus cloud.

It was around seven thirty when he arrived at the airport. Steve was waiting for him and went to greet him as he parked. "Sorry to drag you out, but you've got to see this." The two men walked toward the hangar, where a plane that looked as if it had been in combat sat.

"Holy shit," Tim said. "What happened here?"

"Tim, this is Stan Brady, the pilot who flew this plane in earlier today."

"What happened?" Tim asked again.

"Don't know. When we hit that cloud you guys sent us into, it almost killed us and everybody on board."

"Wait just a fucking minute!" Tim shouted.

"Hold on, everyone, let's not get off on the wrong foot here," Steve broke in. "We all have to work together to try and find some answers."

"Sorry," Stan said. "I'm still just a bit shaken. I've never been through anything like that in all my years of flying."

"Tim, this is Dimo, the airport's top mechanic."

"Pleased to meet you," Dimo said. "We've taken pictures and samples of the metal from the plane, but I just want you all to have a look around yourselves before the FAA gets here in the morning and limits our access."

The four men inspected the plane in and out before heading to the conference room inside the airport. "Well, gentlemen, what do you think? Steve asked.

"It looks as if someone shot the plane with pellets, but what could have burned the metal right through in some spots, and clearly melted it away in others?" Dimo asked.

"Let me have some of those samples and get back with you tomorrow," Tim said.

"What are you thinking?" Stan asked him.

"Can't say. Just give me a day or so?" Tim took the samples of metal fibers and left.

CHAPTER 10

Sandra Blake almost went into shock herself at first sight of her twin sister. Alicia Blake looked red and blue, her light brown skin seemed faded and broken as if she hadn't used lotion in a year. Her hair was nappy, her eyes glazed and wide as if she'd been smoking crack and popping pills for a week. Sandra ran and hugged her sister. "Alicia, it's me, Sandra. I'm here for you, baby. Can you hear me?"

Alicia just stared with the blankness of no man's land. Sandra wanted to cry, but she knew if there was a shred of weakness in her, her twin sister would pick it up no matter what state of mind she was in, so she held strong. She told her sister, "I'm going to go talk with the doctors right now, and we're going to get you all better and take you home."

Caleb and Sanchez were waiting outside the room when Sandra and the doctor came out. "Now, is someone going to tell me what the shit happened?" she demanded.

"There was a terrible accident, if you can call it that," Sanchez said.

"What do you mean by 'if you can call it that'?"

"Well, we have the remains of at least seven other victims as far as we can tell so far. Your sister is the only witness, and she's not talking."

"Are you trying to imply she had something to do with whatever happened out there?"

"No, ma'am, I'm just stating the facts. Now, what do you know about the people she was with on the boat?" He pulled out their IDs. Sandra told him she didn't know any of them. "Well, did your sister have any enemies that you know of?"

"Look here, she was on vacation, Mr. Sancheat."

"Sanchez, Captain Sanchez. Look I know this is hard on you, but what exactly bought you here? We checked the dates your sister and her friends checked in, and you weren't here, so it's really strange how you just happen to show up on the day we get seven people murdered in such a gruesome fashion."

"Murdered?"

"Captain, please let me," Caleb said.

"Sure, go ahead. I'm done for now, but I still have a lot of questions for you, Ms. Blake."

"Likewise," she said. "Now, if you two don't mind, I have a lot of questions for the doctor about Alicia's current condition."

The doctor had no good news for her. Sandra had to get out of this hospital so she could think. She went and kissed her sister goodnight and left.

"Do you need a ride to your room?" the doctor asked.

"No, thank you, I'll walk. I need the air." Sandra left the hospital and started to cry as she walked down the dark, lonely road and then onto the beach. The sound of the sea calmed her for a minute. Then she came upon a nice little café where a small crowd had gathered. They seemed to be so happy. How could this have happened? She walked over, grabbed a seat, and ordered a stiff drink.

Little George, Sugar, Big George, and Lethia were all at the café. B-George was the first to spot her. He saw the tears and, thinking about the island slogan "One Happy Island," said to the rest, "See what I mean? Everybody on this damn island ain't happy. Look at her over there crying and shit like she just lost her man to one of these island girls."

Lethia hit him on the arm. "You need to stop, damn. Yaw can be bad."

Lethia and Sugar went over to Sandra. "Sorry to bother you, but is everything all right?"

"Yes, I would just like to be alone."

"Girl, that looks like the last thing you need right now," Sugar said. "I'm Sugar, this is Lethia. We just got here, and nothing could be more terrifying than what just happened to us."

Sandra could see that they were not going to leave, so she told them, "Let me freshen up a second, ladies, and I'll be right back." She went to the ladies' room and thought of how much she really did need to talk to someone. But could she just spill her guts out to total strangers? They were all Afro-Americans, and all of them appeared to be from the States. She would have a drink with them and listen to what they thought was so terrifying.

Sandra returned. Big G and Little G had moved to her table. She paused and then went and sat down, knowing she was going to need a friend. After listening to their story, Sandra told hers, and they all sat quietly until Little G spoke. "You know, you really need to talk to my brother. He said he had this feeling or premonition that something strange was going on on this island."

CHAPTER 11

Louis got up early the next morning to take a walk down the beach before the sun came up. He always did this any time he would visit the islands. It helped to clear his mind. He was almost out the door when his mother called out, "Hey, you going walking?"

"Yes."

"Wait up, give me five minutes."

Louis waited, and his mom joined him. They had been walking about ten minutes when she told him about Sandra and what she'd told them.

"Damn," he said. "That sounds like the shit I was dreaming about the night before we came here."

CHAPTER 12

Tim Coles had been up half the night digging up all the information he could on nimbostratus clouds. He'd also called a friend of his who had retired from the NASA space program and was now living in Naples, Florida. His name was Jason Pitts, and he was an expert on metal and its physical properties, chemical properties, and electron structure. Tim was sure Jason could help determine what could have possibly melted through the metal of the plane. Tim sent the samples through Express so Jason would get them first thing in the morning. He would call around 1:00 p.m., but now it was time to give today's forecast.

"Now here is our local forecast for Monday, February 15. A chance of showers this morning. Partly cloudy skies in the afternoon, high 87 degrees Fahrenheit. Winds from the east at 10–20 miles per hour. Chance of rain 30 percent. Tonight, variable clouds, with some scattered showers possible overnight. Low near 75 degrees Fahrenheit. Winds at 10–15 miles per hour. Chance of rain 30 percent."

Tim reported the weather conditions for the rest of the week. He couldn't help but wonder where the nimbostratus cloud was and how it picked up those high wind gusts yesterday. "So there's your forecast for the week. Be sure to keep those umbrellas handy. I'll be back with more updates at noon."

It was about 7:30 a.m. when Tim's phone rang. It would be his girlfriend, Marie, telling him the school bus had just left and their daughter was en route to Agnes Kleuterschool. She was in kindergarten. "Are you coming by this morning?" Marie asked.

"Can't, got some extra work I have to do here at the station."

"When will I see you?"

"Sometime this evening," Tim said. "Oh, by the way, did you give Tania the umbrella?"

"No, I forgot. She doesn't have that far to go from the bus to the school, and besides, it's not really coming down that hard. Like you said, just some showers. Really, Tim, it's just rain. How is a little rain going to hurt?"

CHAPTER 13

Sandra Blake was at the hospital early that morning with her sister. The doctors were running more tests. There hadn't been any changes in Alicia's condition. She just lay there with that blank expression on her face, as if she were somewhere else. What had happened out on that boat? Who had killed all those people? Sandra knew her sister was incapable of such an act, so it had to be someone or something else. But why was Alicia spared, out of all the people on that boat? She needed answers, and she was going to need some help. She decided she would see if the other Americans from the café would help.

Lieutenant Caleb and Captain Sanchez were up early this morning as well. They were at the coast guard dock where the *Two of Us* had been towed. Half the island police force was there getting prints, blood samples, bone DNA, and pieces of organs.

"Be sure to get some of those water samples on the deck that haven't completely evaporated. I want answers!" Sanchez shouted.

Sandra had gone to the Alexanders' villa. Louis and his mom were just returning from their walk. The rest of the family was just finishing breakfast. The butler showed her in.

"Good morning, everyone."

"Morning," the family replied.

"How are you this morning?" Sugar asked.

"OK. I was wondering if I could get someone to go down to the docks and the police station with me this morning."

"Sure," Louis said. "I have some things I'm concerned about that seem a bit odd. George, why don't you come with us?"

"All right, let me grab a few things first."

Trish wasn't really crazy about her husband running off with this woman. First, she was very good looking. Sandra Blake had one of those figures most women only dreamed about and all men wished their wives had. But she didn't want to cause a scene in front of the rest of the family, and she knew Sandra needed help and that her husband was really on edge for some reason. Besides, Sugar was letting Little George go, so why couldn't Louis?

Then Louis spoke. "Hey, we'll meet up with you guys at the beach in a couple of hours."

The three of them left, headed for the docks.

CHAPTER 14

It was a beautiful day on the island—no rain yet, and the beaches were full of tourists just enjoying the water and sunshine. On the other side of the island, there was some cloud cover, and it was getting darker. The time was about 11:00 a.m. now, and the children from Agnes Kleuterschool were at lunch. Most were outside in the yard. They were running around, screaming, and playing games when rain started to fall. Their screams became shrieks of pain and of horror as rain pelted them from above. They were all running now, some trampling over the others to get away.

One of the teachers noticed a little girl bleeding, and then another, and another. She dashed outdoors, and she too felt the pain from the burning rain. She screamed for help, and some of the other teachers ran out to get the kids inside. They managed to get all the children inside except for two. One had been burned so badly that he had holes in his clothes and just lay there smoking. The other, a little girl, looked as if someone had just pulled her face out of a pot of hot grease. Both were dead. The children and teachers were all inside now. Everyone had gotten burned, some worse than others.

Little Tania only had a few burns on her arms, but she, like the rest, was more in shock than anything else. What had just happened? Had someone dropped some type of chemical from a plane that passed by? The principal called 911. Ambulances, police, and parents were rushing to the school and hospitals to get their young. The rain had stopped.

*   *   *

Tim Coles was in the middle of his forecast when he got the call from Marie. He too left and headed for the hospital. *What happened?* he wondered all the way there. All Marie had said was that there had been some type of accident at the school and for him to get to the hospital ASAP. Louis, George, and Sandra were pulling up to the dock when the call came. Most of the police left and headed to investigate what happened at the school. Louis noticed some men hosing a boat off and went closer. They were washing off blood.

"Hey, you two, over here," he called out.

"This is it," Sandra said. "This is the boat my sister and her friends were on."

Louis noticed the name on the boat, the *Two of Us*.

"What happened on this boat?" George asked the men.

"Not sure, except they think some bitch went crazy and chopped up her friends," one of the men replied.

Hearing that, Sandra was outraged and was just about to give the man a piece of her mind when Louis grabbed her and shook his head. Then Louis asked the man, "Where did all the police go? They seemed to be in a hurry."

"Yeah." It was the other man who spoke this time. "Something happened at one of the schools, and a bunch of the kids had to be rushed to the hospital. Captain Sanchez was on his way there."

Sandra grabbed Louis and George. "We have to go now, that's where they have my sister."

CHAPTER 15

On the beach, it was mostly sunny, and the rest of the Alexander clan was just enjoying the sunshine. However, there were a few clouds hovering above. One caught the eye of Lou Jr.

"Lazarr, look at that dark cloud way out there. It looks like some kind of flying dragon with a lion's head or something."

"Where?" she said.

"Out there. You see where that dude is parasailing? He's about to go right under it."

About five to seven miles out to sea, you could see a man being pulled by a boat, and they were headed under a low-level cloud, a nimbostratus cloud. He had to be three to five hundred feet in the air above the boat—one could barely see the rope that connected him to what looked like a parachute. Below, on the boat, were a man and a woman drinking beer. They were too busy watching him to see that they were heading right into a cloud that had now started to pour heavy rains. The wind started getting stronger, and the man was being blown all over the place and was trying to signal for them to reel him in.

Then the woman screamed. They were in the rain. She was withering away as soon as the water touched her body. The driver of the boat was screaming too, jerking the steering wheel from side to side. The boat flipped over.

Lou Jr. and Lazarr were watching when the boat flipped. They called out to their mother, "Mom, look! Out there! That boat just flipped over."

"Look, up there."

The man in the air was dangling. Though no one could hear his screams, they knew he was in trouble. His blood was pouring into the sea below. Some of the other tourists were watching now and screaming. Others had run out into the water to get their children. The nimbostratus cloud seemed to have grown or spread out; it was now headed right for the shore. The skeleton remains of the man parasailing dropped into the sea.

There was panic as the people farther out in the water on boats and Jet Skis were now being melted by the burning rain. Some had almost outrun the fast-moving cloud. One man, who opted to try to get to shore but decided to outrun it by width, ran into a woman who had been snorkeling and took her head clean off. He then crashed into a sailboat. The Jet Ski and boat exploded.

The Alexanders were all in the van, now speeding through traffic. Sugar was driving, and Lethia was screaming at her, telling her to watch where she was going. She kept turning around looking for the clouds. Lazarr was shouting for her to go faster. Lou. Jr. was trying to tell them the rain had stopped and the cloud had gone back out to sea. Trish was holding on to Brie who was crying. That's when Sugar sideswiped an oncoming car, and the van flipped over and ended up in a ditch.

Big George never made it back to the van. He was in the hotel when all the panic started and never saw what happened. He just saw people running for their lives in a state of shock, so he stayed where he was at the hotel bar. He stopped one woman and asked her what had happened, but she was in pain and bleeding, as a couple of drops had gotten her. She could only point to the sky.

Big George hoped the rest of the family was safe. He'd been looking for a couple of hours now and could find no one. It was time to check back at the villa. They had to be there, waiting and just as worried as him. He got a cab and was on his way back when he saw the van lying in the ditch.

"Pull over!" he shouted. There was no sign of any of them. "Where's the hospital? Take me there now and hurry."

CHAPTER 16

Jason Pitts was in Naples, Florida, looking at the metal samples Tim Coles had sent. This was strange. The metal gave the appearance of having been burned, but what could burn through this type of metal, especially while a plane was in flight or, as Tim had said, passing through a rain cloud? There was also a wet, slimy, sticky substance that had affixed itself to the metal that he had not yet analyzed. He would have to go to the space center for that. The space center wasn't that far. If he left now, he'd be back by noon and could tell Tim of his findings.

At the space center, Jason Pitts was astonished at his findings. This could not be. Attached to the metal was some type of parasite, one that he was not familiar with. It was still alive, eating its way through the metal. Jason borrowed some equipment from the space center and headed home. He needed to get in touch with Tim and do some more research on where this thing had come from. He also wanted to check out all the latest shuttle activity for the past year. He also removed a piece of wreckage from the latest shuttle disaster, the space shuttle *Columbia*.

CHAPTER 17

At the hospital, there was total chaos. The children from Agnes Kleuterschool, their parents, the police, and the media were all at the hospital looking for loved ones and trying to get answers. The hospital was terribly understaffed and not prepared for the crunch.

The Alexanders were among the last to be admitted. Tim Coles was their looking for Marie and his daughter. Louis, Sandra, and George had just arrived. Big George pulled up in the cab. Luis Sanchez had just gotten the call about what had happened on the beach. It was all over the news now—"Chemical warfare kills dozens and injures hundreds at school and beach. Island sprayed with toxic chemicals." They were all trying to guess what could have happened.

The hospital staff had to redirect the beach victims to the hospital on the other side of the island. *What is happening here?* Louis thought to himself. Could this be what he'd been dreaming about?

They were just about to go check on Sandra's sister when Big George came up. "Where are they?" he asked. "Are they OK?"

"Who?" Louis replied.

"Your mother and the rest of the family. They were in an accident. I found the van flipped over in a ditch. My guess is they were trying to outrun the clouds."

"What?" Louis and Little George both said.

"Go find your family," Sandra said. "I have to check on my sister. I'll catch up with you guys later." She got in the elevator.

Louis turned around and spotted Lazarr going into one of the rooms.

"There," he said. "Come on." The three men went into the room where Louis had just seen his daughter go into, and the whole family was there. He hugged his wife. "Is everyone OK?"

"Yes, we're all OK," she answered, "just a little cut and bruised."

The doctor was still in the room. "Well, everyone appears to be all right, but I'd like to run some more tests."

"Thank you, doctor, but no thanks," Lethia said. "We just want to get back to our villa. You can give us something for pain and headaches, but we're not staying here."

"Mom, are you sure?" Louis said.

"Yes, we have to get to the villa now."

They got some prescriptions from the doctor and left. The hospital was still in a chaotic mess. Children were crying and moaning. Parents were screaming for doctors to treat their children. The police were questioning the teachers about what had happened. Some family members of the dead were being asked to try and identify their loved ones' bodies.

Sandra was with her sister now, who, in all the chaos going on, still sat with a blank stare, totally unchanged from whatever had happened out on the boat. Could they have run into whatever these people at the hospital ran into? There were quite a few of the children with that same blank stare. But what had caused this? Was the island under attack? All Sandra knew was that her sister wasn't showing any signs of improvement, and she had to get her out of this damn hospital and back to the States. No time better than the present. Who would notice with all the commotion going on? Surely, the Alexanders would put them up until she could find out what was really going on. Sandra got Alicia dressed and walked her right out of the hospital.

Sanchez sent Caleb to the hospital on the other side of the island, where things were no different. Tim Coles found Marie and his daughter and took them home.

CHAPTER 18

Jason Pitts was back in Naples now. The time was 2:00 p.m. It had taken him longer than he'd thought, but Tim had not tried to call. Jason was in his basement, which was actually a research lab. Jason set up his stuff and was about to run a few more tests when the phone rang.

"Hello, Jason, it's Tim. What can you tell me? Because we have some very strange shit happening all over the island."

"Well, Tim, to be honest, I'm not quite sure what this is. I need to run a few more tests and cross-reference some types of metal and bacteria samples."

"Bacteria? What has that got to do with any of this? My daughter was almost burned or mutilated by some type of chemical that fell from the sky or that was sprayed out of the sky. At the beach, the same thing. We've got dead and injured people all over the island, and you're talking about some bacteria?"

"Calm down, Tim. Give me two hours, and I assure you, I'll have some answers for you."

Tim was about to say something else when he heard the dial tone. "Dammit."

The sheriff. Tim would get some answers from him. No, he was probably swarmed with people wanting answers just like him.

Jason Pitts didn't mention the parasite. There was no telling what else the parasite or parasites that were literally eating through the metal samples from the plane were capable of. Now he was looking very closely at a few of the metal fragments from the space shuttle *Columbia*.

"My god, no," Jason said. "It can't be."

At that moment, his doorbell rang. Who could it be? Then the back door. There was no time left. He sent Tim a quick e-mail, deleted it, and hid the samples from the plane and shuttle. As he turned around, two men entered the lab.

"Who are you, and how did you get in here?" Jason asked.

A tall white man who weighed about 250 pounds slapped Jason. He fell to the floor. Then the other man, a short, stocky white man, kicked him in the ribs and said, "I'll ask the questions here. Pick him up and sit him in the chair over there."

"Would you like a drink, Mr. Pitts? I know I'm dying for one."

"Upstairs in the front cabinet," Jason said as he spit out a gulp of blood.

A few minutes later, the tall man returned with a bottle of Jack Daniel's and two glasses. The shorter one poured himself a drink and then Jason one. Then he said, "My friend here doesn't like to drink on the job. Mr. Pitts, permit me to introduce myself. My name is Lester Creed."

CHAPTER 19

Captain Sanchez and Lieutenant Caleb were back at the police station.

"Caleb, let's look at the facts. None of this shit with the mutilated bodies started until we got that distress call from the *Two of Us*, correct?"

"That's right, sir."

"And that's the same time when the Blake sisters showed up on our friendly island, correct?"

"That's right, sir, but—"

Sanchez cut him off. "Wait, hear me out. I did a background check on Ms. Sandra Blake, and get this, she works for NASA. At first I was sure it was drug related. Do you remember about three years ago, NASA wanted to use our fly zone to do some type of testing?"

"Yes, but why would she involve her sister?"

"That's just it. Something went wrong. Caleb, call the hospital and see if there's been any change in her sister's condition."

Caleb made the call. "Sir, you're not going to believe this: the sister's gone."

"Gone? What do you mean she's gone?"

"Turns out, during the confusion, she disappeared."

"Bullshit, not in her condition. Come on, let's get over to that resort."

At the resort, there was nothing. The clerk told the officers that Sandra had picked up her sister's things and checked out.

"How did this happen?" Sanchez demanded. "Where is the officer that was on watch?"

"Sir, in all that happened today, he got pulled. The whole force was split between the hospitals, the school, and the beach."

"Fuck, check the airport. See if they got out. With traffic and the time, it would be close to impossible, so I'm positive they're still on the island. Then check all the hotels and resorts."

"Captain, you know how long that's going to take?"

"Lieutenant, are you fucking busy now?"

"Yes, sir. Right away, sir."

CHAPTER 20

At the villa, the Alexanders were just sitting down for dinner when security came into the dining room. The cook had prepared jerk chicken, a tossed salad, and fried corn. Carl the butler motioned for Louis. "Sorry to interrupt your dinner, but there is someone here that says you are a friend and they need to speak to you immediately."

Louis turned around to see Sandra and her sister, who was just staring blankly. "My god, is everything OK?"

"I'm not sure. I had to get her out of that hospital. I didn't know where else to go."

Trish and Sugar walked in. "What's going on?" Trish demanded before she saw Alicia.

"It's fine," Louis said. By now, the rest of the family was in the living room with them.

"This is my sister I told you all about," Sandra explained. "I had to get her out of there. I didn't know where else to go."

"Come on in, baby, we were just about to have dinner, and you look starved," Lethia told them. "Come on, everyone, before the food gets cold."

The butler brought two more plates, and Lethia said grace. Louis and Little George were drinking Merlot. Louis Jr. was staring at Alicia and finally broke the silence. "What's wrong with her?"

Lazarr kicked him under the table.

"Stop!" Lou Jr. shouted. "I just—"

"It's OK," Sandra said. "Let me explain."

"Wait," Lethia jumped in. "Eat your food." She motioned for the cook and told her to fix up one of those protein drinks for Sandra's sister since she was unresponsive to regular food. After dinner, Sugar put Brie to bed. She was too young to understand what was going on. Hell, at this point, nobody understood. The Alexanders, along with Sandra and her sister, went outside under the gazebo with a couple more bottles of Merlot.

Alicia Blake just sat in her daze, and then Sandra told the Alexanders what she knew up to this point, and how Captain Sanchez blamed her and Alicia.

Since Lou Jr. was the first to spot the terror on the beach, he told everyone what he saw.

"That's crazy," his sister said.

"No, wait a minute," Big George broke in. "One of the ladies at the beach was pointing to the sky."

"See? Told you, clouds," Lou Jr. said.

"Oh please," Lazarr replied. "The clouds."

"No, wait a minute, everyone, this is going to sound like something off the Syfy channel, but before we ever got here, I started dreaming about screaming, rain, and mostly something about the clouds," Louis told them.

Big George gave a chuckle, and then Little George jumped in. "No, he's right on the plane. Louis, don't you remember I told you I had dreamed something about the clouds too?"

"Oh, come on," Sugar said. "The clouds? Yaw need to put those drinks down and leave that bud alone."

"No, wait a minute," Louis said. "You all just said there was a monstrous cloud on the beach, it has to have something to do with it."

"I agree with my dad," Lou Jr. said.

"All right then. So, assuming this has any bearing, what do we do now?" Trish asked.

"The plane. We should check out what really happened to the plane," Louis said. "You remember the dark cloud we flew through on our way here?"

"Yes," everyone agreed. Lazarr said, "What about the weatherman? He should have some records of strange clouds or something like that."

"She's right, they should," her mom said.

"There's one more thing," Sandra said. "I need to get Alicia back to the States. She can't be left alone here."

"But how?" Little George asked. "Cops gotta be looking for you two."

Louis had been noticing how much Sandra and Sugar resembled each other—same complexion, same build. They could fix the hair, but what about Alicia? He would sleep on it. "I have an idea," he said. "Give me till the morning to work it out. In the meantime, I think it best to just chill for the night."

Everyone agreed and turned in. Louis stayed out, thinking of what was happening and how to stop it. It had been two hours, and he was still outside and just about to go in when Sandra came back out.

"Hi," she said.

"Hey," Louis said. "I was just about to go in."

"Could you stay for a few more minutes? I need to tell you something that I don't think your whole family was ready for."

Louis poured himself another drink and then Sandra one. "OK, Sandra. What is it?"

She broke down in tears. Louis stood up and then stood her up. He put his arms around her, gave her a long hug, and told her everything was going to be all right. Louis didn't see his wife watching from the upstairs balcony. Sandra gave him a peck on his cheek, told him how sweet his family was, sat down, and began to tell Louis about her position at NASA and how she knew about certain classified experiments the USA wanted to test in the Caribbean.

"I think this could be connected in some type of way," she said.

Louis told her about his background in biochemistry and then suggested they both get some sleep. Trish was up waiting for him when he got upstairs. She was visibly upset. "What the hell is going on between you and that woman?"

"What do you mean? There's nothing going on."

"Then why were you kissing her?"

"What, honey? What are you talking about? No one was kissing anyone."

"Are you going to stand here and tell me I didn't see you kiss that woman?"

"That's right. I was trying to comfort her. She kissed me on the cheek to thank us for our help. Are you that insecure?" Louis felt his wife's palm bounce off his face. Then she jumped on the bed and started crying. Louis left found an empty room and went to sleep.

CHAPTER 21

Lester Creed was a hired henchman for NASA and the Pentagon who made sure that their employees never went public with the fuckups at the two government facilities. He had killed men and women who had tried, and he made their families disappear too. NASA had called him when they saw the tape of Jason Pitts removing scraps from the space shuttle *Columbia*.

Lester Creed and his man had beaten Jason really bad, and he knew they were going to kill him, so he was determined not to tell them anything.

"All right, Mr. Pitts. This is the last time I'm going to ask you. If you don't tell me what I want to know, I'm going to take you to alligator row, hang you from the bridge, and feed you to the gators. *Where are the scraps from the shuttle?*"

Jason spit blood in his face, and Creed slapped him so hard that he knocked him and the chair he was tied to clear across the room.

"Get his car, put him in the trunk, and follow me to the gators. We'll come back and search the house."

Chapter 22

Tim Coles had received Jason's e-mail and had been calling for hours when he decided he would just fly to Naples. He felt there was something terribly wrong and felt sickened because he had involved Jason in it. He told Marie he would be leaving around 1:00 p.m. the next day.

Marie questioned why he had to go. Tim told her the lives of the people in Aruba depended on what he might find there. Then he called Steve from air traffic control and told him to hold off the FAA until he could get back the next day.

CHAPTER 23

The next morning, Louis was on his way out of the door when his mother and brother joined him. They decided they needed to meet with Tim ASAP, so Louis set up a meeting at nine. Tim had insisted it be early since he was flying out in the afternoon. While walking, Louis told them about the fight with his wife last night.

His brother said, "Can you blame her? The woman is fine as hell."

"Yeah, I know, but I didn't do shit."

The rest of the family was just sitting down for breakfast—all except Trish, who just wanted to go home. Sandra and Alicia were at the table too when Louis, his brother, and his mom got back from their walk. After breakfast and a shower, Louis, Little George, Lou Jr., and Sandra went to see Tim Coles.

* * *

Lester Creed and his man arrived at alligator row and, as promised, hung Jason Pitts from the bridge. The gators went on a feeding frenzy, leaping out of the swampy waters and snatching the bottom half of Jason's body apart like twigs. He screamed and begged for mercy until he passed out from the pain. He was still alive when Lester finished his cigar and cut the rope. The top half of his torso fell in the swamp, and the gators fought over his remains until there was no more of Jason Pitts. The two men returned to Jason's home and ransacked it but were unable to find the shuttle scraps. Lester took the computer, bugged the house, set up some cameras, and left.

"We'll have to get his phone records from the phone company. I'm sure he told someone where the scraps are." The two men left.

CHAPTER 24

When the Alexanders arrived at the TV station, Tim was waiting for them. The five of them went into his office and exchanged stories. Tim had been right—all of them were right. There was something in the clouds. Tim agreed to help get Alicia out of the country. He needed Sandra to help him find his way in the States. He called Dimo the mechanic to help get Sandra and her sister on the plane without being noticed by the police. They flew into Fort Lauderdale, rented a car, dropped Alicia at a private clinic, and drove to Naples.

There was nothing the Alexanders could do but try to enjoy their vacation and stay out of the rain until the two returned with what was hidden in Jason Pitts's house. The sky was clear, and there were no clouds, so Louis, his son, and his brother went Jet Skiing while the rest of the family just hung around the villa. The brothers decided they would try to get the ladies out of the villa that night and go to one of the hot spots on the island, Carlos 'n Charlie's, for some dancing and drinks.

CHAPTER 25

Lester Creed and his man were at NASA, waiting for any helpful information from Jason Pitts's computer to be retrieved. One of the interns walked into the spy room where Creed was. The spy room was just that—it had bugging devices, cameras, computer taps, and satellite search set up all over the world so the government could watch and hear your every move. Lester Creed was watching Jason Pitts's house for any activity.

"What do you have for me?" he asked the intern.

"Sorry, there's nothing there, sir. The computer's hard drive has been destroyed."

"Destroyed how?" Creed demanded. "I know he was using it when we got there. It was still warm."

"Well, sir, he probably just placed a magnet on the side of the PC tower. That would immediately destroy the hard drive."

"Fuck!" Creed shouted. He motioned for the intern to leave, and then turned to his man. "Anything from the phone company yet?"

"No, sir. They said it would take at least twenty-four hours."

"Twenty-four hours? We don't have that kind of time. We have to find out who he was working with before any of that classified information about what really happened to the shuttle gets out."

Before Creed could get out another word, his man pointed to the monitors and said, "Sir, isn't that Pitts's house?"

Lester Creed swung his chair around. On the monitor, you could see a car pulling up into the driveway. A man and a woman got out of the car, went to the front door, and started knocking.

"Get me a unit over there now," Creed blurted. "Have them stay back. Do not engage, just listen and watch. Also, get me a satellite fix on that car, and pictures of those two. I want to know everything about them and their families right now. And get our van ready."

"Yes, sir." Creed's man picked up the phone and relayed his orders. And then the two of them were on their way to the late Jason Pitts's house.

CHAPTER 26

In Aruba, it was quiet. Louis, his son, and his brother had decided to go on a boat tour after they had finished Jet Skiing. They decided they would learn how to snuba. Snuba was in between snorkeling and scuba diving. You could go 20 to 30 feet underwater. The difference was instead of the air tanks being on your back, they were on top of the water inside a raft. The air hoses were connected to the mouthpiece and the tanks, so you could swim freely and still breathe. There was a sunken ship they would explore this afternoon.

The ladies had decided to go downtown and do some shopping, including Trish. The skies were clear all over the island, and the forecast didn't predict any rain that day, so everyone felt pretty safe going out and about. They had all agreed that at the first sign of rain, they would take cover.

CHAPTER 27

Lieutenant Caleb's search for Sandra and her sister was getting him nowhere. He and the officers assisting him had covered all the hotels on the island and were now starting to search the resorts and villas. Caleb pulled up to Endless Summer, the Alexanders' villa. All of the Alexander family was gone. Sandra and her sister were back in the States. Caleb was showing the sisters' picture to the Endless Summer staff when Carl the butler told him that both the sisters had been there. He told him he didn't know if they were still with the Alexanders, but the family usually ate supper around six thirty. Caleb called the rest of the officers and told them to end their search, and then he called the captain, who told him to return to the station. Both of them would pay the Alexanders a visit at suppertime.

CHAPTER 28

Sandra Blake and Tim Coles had taken her sister to the Crisis Stabilization Center for Trauma Victims in Fort Lauderdale. There had not been a lot of change in her condition, except she would now follow the doctor's pen with her eyes from side to side. Tim and Sandra had gotten no answer from the door. In the e-mail Jason sent Tim, there were instructions on how to get in the house. Tim and Sandra went to the backyard. Taped under the diving board was a key to the house. They entered through the back door.

Lester Creed's men who were watching the house called Lester. "They're in the house, sir. What would you like us to do?"

"Nothing, just stay where you are," Lester told them as he watched the two from his moving van. He was about twenty minutes away.

Inside the house, Tim and Sandra could see blood on the floor, where Jason had been beaten.

"Search upstairs for Jason while I get the scraps," Tim told Sandra. Jason's e-mail had told him where the scraps were. They were hidden in a secret room behind the bookshelf.

"Dammit!" Creed shouted as he watched Tim retrieve the metal scraps from the shuttle. He wasn't sure about the other package that Tim grabbed.

"What do you think is in the box?" Creed's man asked.

"Don't know."

"Do you want our men to move in now that they have the scraps, sir?"

"No."

* * *

Sandra returned from upstairs.

"He's not here," she told Tim, and then asked, "What's that?" Then she put her hand over her mouth. "We have to get out of here now," she whispered to Tim.

"Right now?" Tim could see the fear starting to consume Sandra. It was the package he was holding, not the box.

"Come on, now," Sandra whispered. Tim and Sandra hurried to the car and sped off.

"Where to?" Tim asked. "And what's wrong?"

"Who lives at that house and what is he doing with this?"

"My friend, Jason Pitts. What is it? It's not what I sent him. What I sent him is in the box. Metal samples from the plane."

"Well, Mr. Coles, what you have there are fragments from the space shuttle *Columbia*, and it's classified top secret. This puts our lives in grave danger. Whatever happened at your friend's house I'm sure was because of it. We have to take it back. More importantly, how did he get it?"

Tim explained that Jason had retired from the Kennedy Space Center and was an expert on metal types.

"You have to be kidding me," Sandra said. "That's where I work. Well, I'm on loan to them for now, and that's what we were working on. The Shuttle disaster."

"We can't take it back. Jason may have given his life for it, and the lives of everyone in Aruba are at stake. I have to find a safe place to examine just what he found."

"Well, nowhere in the States is safe, mister. We have to get this stuff back to Aruba, so how do you suppose we do that?"

"We'll ship it back, go to a FedEx." Tim didn't see the van following them with Jason Creed and his man.

"There's a FedEx up the road a little. We can ship it, and then I have to go to the space center. There are a few things we're going to need," Sandra told him.

"Don't you think that's going to be a little dangerous?" Tim asked.

"It's too late for that now. We're already in over our heads, and trust me, more people are going to die."

Tim and Sandra pulled up to the FedEx and shipped the packages overnight. There was a truck about to leave, so the clerk sent it out with that load.

Creed didn't see the truck leave. He was too busy giving his people orders. "Get prints from the house, take the cameras, debug the place, and burn it," he told the men who were still at the house.

Tim and Sandra left the FedEx and headed for the space center. They were about twenty minutes away. Lester Creed and his man went into the FedEx office. There was only one clerk working. Creed locked the door behind him and put the closed sign on the window.

The clerk asked, "What's going on? You can't do that. Who are you people?"

Creed's man pulled out a gun and slapped the clerk upside his head. "Shut up."

Lester Creed grabbed the man by his collar and pulled him almost over the counter. "I'm going to ask you a few questions, you are going to answer them. Understand?"

"Yes," the bleeding clerk said.

"Now, where is the package that couple dropped off, and where are they trying to send it to?"

The clerk tried to lie. "They didn't drop off anything, they were just checking on prices."

Creed pulled out a knife and stabbed the clerk's hand into the counter. "You dare insult my intelligence, you little shit. Search the place, find the package," he told his man.

Creed's man was unable to find the package. "It's not here, sir. Looks like it's headed to Aruba."

Creed taped the clerk's mouth. The two men set the place on fire with the clerk stuck to the counter and left. Back in the van, Creed called his satellite patrol. "Where are they?"

"Headed to the space center," a voice said.

Creed looked puzzled, wondering why they would be going there. Then he spoke. "Enough of this bullshit. We'll engage them at the center. Hurry, let's go."

CHAPTER 29

It was around six o'clock when the Alexander women returned from shopping and started to freshen up for dinner. Louis, Lou Jr., and George had not returned but were en route. Big George had spent his day alone at the beach, just reading and napping. On his way to his room, he ran into Carl the butler, who told him of the visit from the police and how they would probably be coming back. At that moment, Louis, his brother, and his son walked in.

"Hey, what's happening?" Louis said to Big George.

"We may have a problem. The police were here earlier looking for the twins."

"What did you tell them?"

"Nothing," George said. "I wasn't here. They spoke to Carl."

Little George asked, "What did Carl tell them?"

"He told them that the twins had been here," Big George replied.

"OK," Louis said. "Everyone, get together in fifteen minutes. I'm going to take a quick shower before dinner, and we can get this straight before they get here."

Everyone was outside by the pool when Louis came back out feeling refreshed from his shower. He had thought hard about what the police wanted and remembered that Sandra had told him the captain thought she and her sister had something to do with the deaths on the *Two of Us*. He reminded his family of that, and they all agreed not to share what they thought was happening on the island or tell of the twins' whereabouts.

About fifteen minutes into their meal, Sanchez and Caleb popped up. Carl led them into the dining room where the family was enjoying dinner. Carl announced the officers. "Sorry to interrupt your meal, but you have visitors."

"Thank you," Sanchez told Carl. "Good evening. Sorry to interrupt your meal. I'm Captain Sanchez, and this is Lieutenant Caleb. We need to ask you a few questions about these two ladies," he said as he pulled out their picture.

Louis took the picture and said, "Why? What have they done?"

"Excuse me, I didn't get your names," Sanchez said. "You are?"

"We are the Alexanders from USA," Louis answered, "and I asked what they have done and what it has got to do with my family that you two have to interrupt our dinner?"

"Mr. Alexander, there's no need to be hostile. We are conducting an investigation, and we understand the sisters were here at the villa."

"That's right. They were here a couple of nights ago. They had dinner with us. Is that a crime on your island? Are you telling us we can't come in contact with other people while we're here on our vacation?"

"No, sir, it's not, and I wish you would calm down. We just have a few more questions. Does anyone here know of their whereabouts now or where they may be staying?"

"No, captain, and unless you are going to arrest us for sharing our table with them, I suggest you and your lieutenant leave now. Carl!" Louis shouted.

"Yes, sir?" Carl said as he reappeared.

"Please show the officers to the door."

"Yes, sir."

"We'll be in touch, Mr. Alexander," Sanchez said as he grabbed an apple from the table and headed out the door with Caleb following.

"That was just great, Louis," his wife said. "I don't see why we couldn't just tell them what we know and let them handle it. That is their job, but no, we have to stick our neck out for some bitch and her sister who may have killed those people that we know nothing about.

Fuck this bullshit!" Trish hollered as she got up from the table and stormed out the room. Her daughter Lazarr followed.

Sugar asked, "What was that all about?"

"Nothing," Louis replied as he grabbed a bottle of wine and headed outside for the gazebo. "Nothing at all."

*   *   *

Everyone was scattered about the villa when Little George came and sat down with his brother.

"You OK?" he asked.

"Yeah, fine. Just need some air. I know Sugar wanted to know what was going on. What did you tell her?"

"Shit, I just told her about the peck on the cheek and the fight, but it's not your fault, bro. Sugar and Ma were the ones who befriended Sandra in the first place, not you. Hell, you weren't even there."

"Yeah, I know. Hey, I have to get out of here. Going to head to the casino. We'll go clubbing another night. Want to come?"

"Nah, it's supposed to rain. You sure you want to go?"

"Yeah, have to get some air."

"All right, but don't get caught in the rain, bro."

"I won't. See you later." Louis left the villa and headed for the casino. There was no rain. Maybe the weather people were wrong. He knew he shouldn't be out, but he was mad that his wife didn't trust him, so he kept going and prayed he didn't get caught in the rain.

CHAPTER 30

Tim and Sandra arrived at the space center. "What exactly is it that you need from here?" Tim asked.

"I have to get some files and disks out of my office, and we need to find out just what your friend did while he was here. Once we get in, just follow me. Don't speak to anyone. I'm going to have to tap into the main computer to find out where your friend was, and then we have to go there and check out what he found out, and if there's a connection to what's happening in Aruba."

"What about this stuff? Should we leave it in the car?" Tim asked.

"No way. Your friend is probably already dead. That's our only chance of leverage if we get caught, and I pray we don't." Sandra reached into her purse and pulled out two cards. "Once we go in, do as I do. We have to pass through security. I keep this dummy card and code just in case."

"In case of what?"

"In case of a day like today, Mr. Coles."

*   *   *

Lester Creed was still outside in his van, waiting for Tim's and Sandra's backgrounds and pictures to come though. He had not seen them clearly enough at the house and needed the pictures so he could positively identify them once inside. "Dammit, what's taking them so long? They already been inside for five minutes. We don't have time to—"

"It's coming through now boss," Lester's man cut in.

"Fax the pictures to all security posts, entrances, and exits! Let's move now!" Creed shouted.

* * *

Sandra downloaded some files about the shuttle accident on her computer. She then tapped into the main computer to see where Jason Pitts had been working from in the building.

"Got it, it's just around the corner from here. Come on, let's go."

Creed and his man were inside Sandra's office. "Looks like we just missed them," his man said.

Sandra was downloading what Jason had been working on when he was at the center, and then there was a knock on the door. "Quiet," she said to Tim as you could hear someone trying to get in. Then the door opened. It was a guard. Tim was about to jump him from behind when Sandra said, "No, Tim, don't." Tim lowered the statue he was about to strike the guard with.

"Sean," Sandra said. "What are you doing here?"

"No time for that now. Come on, Creed and his boy are on to you and headed this way. Come on now, hurry." Sean was one of the security guards who got the fax of Sandra. He had a slight crush on her. Sandra had always talked and joked with Sean. He was really a cool guy, she had thought, but she didn't date people at the workplace, so they just became good friends. Sean took them outside, gave her his car, and told her to get as far away as possible. He had heard about Creed and his man and knew that whatever he was after Sandra for, if he caught her, he would never see her again. She kissed him, told him thank you, and sped off.

Creed and his man saw that there was no one at Sean's post and waited. Sean came around the corner.

"Where have you been?" Creed barked. "Why did you leave your post? Didn't you get the fax and call telling you we were looking for these two?" He held up Tim's and Sandra's pictures.

"Yeah, I got it, but I had to piss. But don't worry, no one came this way."

"I hope not, son, for your sake." Creed went to his spy room. "Play back the tape and see where that guard really went to."

"Here it is now, sir." The tape showed the guard helping Sandra and Tim get away. "Should I go get the guard, sir?"

"No need, we'll deal with him later. Call in the security agents at the airport. Get these pictures to them. I want every passenger on their way to Aruba checked, and when they see those two, detain them. Let's go."

Creed and his man headed for the airport.

CHAPTER 31

At the villa, Trish and Sugar were having a glass of wine under the gazebo. Trish told Sugar about what she had seen the other night between Louis and Sandra and how he'd told her it was nothing. She was really scared of the events that had happened.

"I just want off this island before something happens to us."

"I understand how you're feeling, but what if this thing is not just here on the island? What if it happens in the States and we had the chance to stop it and save thousands of lives? I couldn't live with myself knowing that, could you? Then there's the thing about Sandra's sister and what happened out there on that boat. Let's face it, Trish, we're involved, no matter if we chose to be or not, as long as we are on this island. And I, for one, do plan on getting home safe. Think about it, girl. I don't think your husband would wait and come on vacation to start an affair with his whole family around. I think it was just what he told you."

"You're probably right, but why can't we just tell the police what we know? If the twins are innocent, it will come out."

"Trish, did you see her sister? Something horrible happened to her. What if it was one of us? Wouldn't you want to know what the shit was really going on? I'll tell you what I think. I think it's going to get worse until someone puts a stop to it, and that may have to be us."

Sugar got up, grabbed Trish's hand, and told her everything was going to be fine. Then she left.

Trish drank another glass of wine and thought about calling the police, telling them what the family thought was going on and leaving the island. Then it hit her: what proof did they have? They would think she was crazy. She'd have to think of another way, but she was not staying on that island for the rest of the vacation. She was going to come up with something and leave.

CHAPTER 32

Dimo had contacted Stan, who was flying the last flight out of Miami to Aruba that night. Stan had gotten some extra pilot and stewardess uniforms, and he had Tim and Sandra put them on. They got on the plane undetected. Creed was furious that no one spotted them, but he was also on the plane. Neither Tim nor Sandra left the cockpit during the flight. They arrived in Aruba without being found out. "What now?" Creed's man asked.

"We go to the FedEx pickup and check on those packages and where they're headed or who picked them up."

Dimo had already grabbed the packages and had them safe until Tim could retrieve them. In the meantime, Tim and Sandra finally made their way through the airport without being noticed, and they headed to Tim's house, where Dimo would deliver the packages.

Sanchez still had officers at the airport, so when Creed started inquiring about the packages and showing pictures of Tim and Sandra, he was notified. Sanchez and Caleb went to the airport to meet Creed and his man.

CHAPTER 33

Louis was at the casino getting drunk. He was winning in blackjack and had won about $500. It was around 2:00 a.m. when he decided to leave. It started to rain. Louis was at the door trying to stop people from going out in the rain. They laughed at him and called him a drunk. When they went out in the rain and nothing happened, he felt silly and wondered why nothing had happened. Too drunk to make sense of his own rambling, he took a taxi back to the villa and passed out on the couch. His wife came downstairs and saw him strewn across the couch and knew he was drunk. She wondered why she was still with him. Back home, he would often stay out late and come in drunk. They hadn't been intimate. She wondered if he was having an affair. She again wanted off the island and thought of going to the police, and then she broke out in tears and went to bed. It was early when Little George found his brother slumped half on the couch and half on the floor. He woke him up. "Damn, man, you all right?"

Louis opened his eyes, grabbed his head, and said, "Yeah, I'm OK."

"You look like shit. Any luck at the casino?"

"Yeah," Louis said, sitting up. "About five hundred." He got up and went to the bathroom, his brother following him. "Did we bring the Alka-Seltzer?"

"In the cabinet."

Louis drank two tablets and then washed his face. He headed for the kitchen, cut up an apple, and drank a glass of tomato juice. He went upstairs to change into his workout shorts and T-shirt, and then he and his brother went for an early-morning walk and swim in the sea. The rest of the family came down and had breakfast as usual—all except Trish. She was upstairs on the phone.

CHAPTER 34

Creed and his man had left the airport before Captain Sanchez and Lieutenant Caleb had gotten there, but their men followed them to one of the resorts where they had checked in. There was a knock at Creed's door that morning. Creed and his man were already up and just about to head out. Creed grabbed his gun went to the door. "Who is it?" he asked without opening the door.

"Captain Sanchez of the Aruba Police, please open the door."

Creed put his gun in his back and opened the door. Sanchez introduced Lieutenant Caleb and asked, "May we come in? I understand you're looking for these two people." Sanchez held up the pictures of Tim Coles and Sandra Blake.

"Sure, captain, come in."

Caleb was watching Creed's man and put his hand on his gun. Creed's man did the same. Creed was about to pull something out of his back pocket when Sanchez drew his gun, as did Creed's man and Lieutenant Caleb.

"Hold on, everyone, just getting my badge," Creed said as he slowly pulled out his badge. "I'm Special Agent Lester Creed from NASA, and this is my partner Damon. Everyone put their guns up, please."

Sanchez, Caleb, and Damon all holstered their guns. Creed turned to Sanchez. "Now, what can we do for you, captain?"

Creed and Damon were licensed killers and would kill Sanchez and Caleb in a heartbeat if he thought they knew too much.

Sanchez again held up the pictures and asked, "Why are you looking for these two? And even more importantly, you have no jurisdiction in this country, so you are not allowed to carry those weapons. They should have been checked in."

Creed told him they were suspects in a homicide and may have stolen property that was classified from the USA. "We would like your assistance in locating these two. Why are you so interested in them?"

"Well, we've had some accidents on the island, and this woman and her sister are our prime suspects," Sanchez told him, "but it appears they eluded us if you're tracking her from the States."

"Where does Tim fit into all this?" Caleb asked.

"Who is Tim, and what is this you say about this woman having a sister?" Creed said, almost as if he were demanding information now.

"Well, Tim is one of the local weathermen here on the island, and Ms. Blake has a twin sister who was at the scene of the ongoing investigation being conducted," Sanchez told them.

"We need to find this Tim Coles and Ms. Blake right away, so if you could give me his home address," Creed said.

"First, like I said, gentlemen, you will have to be cleared through the prime minister's office for your firearms. Until then, you'll have to surrender them to me," Sanchez told them.

"Sorry, no dice. We keep our weapons. We are on a mission of national security to the States. If you have a problem, call your prime minister and have him call the director of NASA. Until then, give us the information of where we can find this Tim Coles and Ms. Blake and anyone they may have been in contact with, or stay out of our way."

Caleb started to draw his weapon, and Sanchez stopped him. "All right, Mr. Creed, I'll do just that. But let it be known, this is my island, and if you step over the wrong line, you'll answer directly to me. Oh, and find them yourself."

Sanchez and Caleb left.

"Fucking cocky bastards. There's something about those two that bothers me. Put a tail on them. We have to get to Tim first and see what his involvement in this whole thing is," Sanchez said.

CHAPTER 35

Dirk Staten was the governor of Aruba, and Sofie Labridge was one of the eight ministers. Sofie headed up the tourist department, Aruba's main source of income. Aruba was fast becoming one of the Caribbean's hot spots, known for its great weather and friendly people. Sofie went to school in the States, at the University of New Orleans.

The carnival was due to start in a couple of days. All the major cruise lines would be coming to port, Sofie made sure of that. She had worked as a planner for the Mardi Gras in New Orleans. The tourists on the cruise ships bought in millions of dollars in revenue each year. Sanchez and Caleb were in the lobby when the governor called them in. Sofie spoke and was about to leave when Sanchez asked her to stay. "This won't take long, Sofie, but I think you should hear this." Sanchez went on to explain about Creed and Damon and the recent events around the island. The governor assured him he would follow up on the information and told Sanchez to keep a close eye on him.

"Look here, Sanchez," Sofie jumped in. "Right now, I need all of your department looking sharp and making sure everyone has a good time at the carnival, not chasing some fucking Americans around the island. I also need you to get a grip on the hookers on the other side of the island so they don't give our carnival a bad name and start attracting johns from all over the world. I trust you will see to it, Mr. Governor."

"Of course, Sofie. Don't worry," the governor replied. Sofie left the governor's office.

He assured Sanchez he would check out Creed. "Now then, fellows, I have another meeting I must get to, so if you will excuse me, I'll contact you later."

Sanchez and Caleb left. "That *bitch*, all she ever thinks about is the fucking carnival and how much money she can make!" Sanchez shouted as they left the building.

"Well, she is a major stockholder in the Marriott, and they are the island's largest hotel chain. What do you expect?" Caleb joked.

Sanchez's phone rang. It was one of the officers he had following Creed. "Sanchez here."

"Sir, I think this guy may have found something on Tim. He's leaving the news station right now."

"Keep tails on him. If he goes near Tim's place, pull him over. We're headed over there now."

Caleb called Tim's house but got no answer. "He's not picking up. We should probably try his girlfriend's place."

"You're right. Let's go."

CHAPTER 36

Louis and George were back at the villa now, sitting at the dining table. Carl entered the room, behind him were Sandra, Tim, his girlfriend, and his daughter. "Finally made it back. How did it go?" Louis asked.

The rest of the family had gathered in the room now, even Trish.

"Not well, I hate to say. Could we talk to you in private for a moment? Sandra said.

"Not a chance in hell," Trish blurted. "How dare you come into our villa and ask to speak with my husband alone?"

"Honey, just wait a second," Louis said.

Tim interrupted, "Look here, folks. What we have to tell you is very important. At least take the children out of the room." Sugar and Marie took their daughters to the next room and asked the maid to stay with them. Trish insisted her kids stay.

"OK, let's have it," Trish demanded.

Tim told them how they feared his friend Jason Pitts was dead. Sandra explained the shuttle scraps, how it was top secret, and she talked about Creed being on their tail, possibly on the island.

"It's not safe for you to stay here. Creed is a killer. We have scraps from both the flight you were on and from the shuttle crash. My friend is a major shareholder in one of the newer hotels here on the island. We need to move everyone there. The hotel has some new wings that are not yet opened. We can get the presidential suites and have the whole floor to ourselves. No one should be able to find us there. The island is solid booked because of the carnival," Tim told them.

"We have everything we need to further examine these scraps, but we need your help, Louis. The rest of you should just act normal and blend in. Oh, and most importantly, there's a nimbostratus cloud in the forecast for this evening. By now, I think we all know to stay away from it and out of the rain."

CHAPTER 37

Tim had gotten the forecast from one on the interns at the station who didn't give him the whole outlook.

One of the cruise ships that had come into port was experiencing some mechanical problems and had to put all the passengers in hotel rooms. The ship was due to leave in two days, one day after the carnival started. This would give the captain and his crew of fifty enough time to sail back to Port Canaveral and get the necessary repairs and be back in time to pick up all the passengers.

About 50 miles out to sea, the sky was getting darker. One cloud was forming what seemed to be strange images. The sky started to rumble. Most of the crew had come up on deck to observe the strange cloud which was now almost directly above them. The captain tried to navigate the ship around the cloud, but it was too late. In an instant, it started to pour.

The crew had no chance. All you could hear were the screams and shrieks of the crew as they were being eaten apart by the raindrops which felt like a hot blaze from hell. It was horrible. The rain was not only disintegrating the men, but it was also eating its way through the ship. This was no ordinary rain. There was something in the raindrops that no one on this planet had ever seen before or knew anything about. Something not of this world. It was growing, becoming more deadly.

This time, the rain didn't stop. The ship was sinking. Some men managed to get their half-eaten, mutilated bodies below. That didn't help either. Whatever was tearing and eating away at them was now spreading within their bodies, even thought they had gotten out of the rain. One of the crewmen was pulling at his eye sockets until he pulled his own eyeballs right out of his skull, only to have the flesh and bones on his hands eaten next.

The screaming came to a stop as the ship sank, and a whirlpool of blood filled the sea for miles. The captain was unable to send a distress call. The ship was scattered about the seafloor in very deep waters. There were no survivors, no bones, no body parts, no ship. Everything that had come under the nimbostratus cloud was gone—everything in the pathway of *the rain clouds of death!*

CHAPTER 38

Alicia Blake was starting to show signs of improvement. She was now beginning to eat and sit up. She still wasn't talking and still had that blank stare. The doctor had been trying to reach Sandra but was unable to get through because of a problem with her cell phone carrier—Sandra was not aware of the problem. He felt that with her near Alicia, she could draw strength from her. At night, she would break out in cold sweats and start shaking. He attributed this to the traumatic experience she'd been through. It was continually replaying itself in her mind, and she was still trapped in that moment, all alone with no one to pull her out. She looked pale and fragile. She'd lost about twenty pounds. There was something else, some kind of other feeling of fear starting to break through.

Alicia started to blink wildly. She suddenly started screaming and pushing the nurse to the floor. The doctor had stepped out of the room, trying to reach Sandra again. When he heard the racket, he approached Alicia slowly. She kicked the doctor in the groin, and he fell to the floor, gasping for air. Two interns ran into the room and grabbed Alicia, forcing her back onto the bed. The doctor, while still on the floor, told the nurse to give her a sedative to put her to sleep and strap her to the bed so she wouldn't be able to hurt herself or anyone else.

Louis, Tim, and Sandra had set up in the back room of one of the suites and were going through Jason Pitts's findings when Sandra got this cold shiver all over her body. She felt scared. She needed to check in on Alicia. She stepped out of the room and pulled out her cell phone to call the clinic. There was no service. Something was wrong. The phone was fully charged and within an area where it should work. She went outside the hotel, near the pool, where she saw the rest of the Alexanders hanging around. Still, no service. She walked over to the payphone, dialed the clinic, and was just about to give the operator her credit card number when she thought of Creed. She hung up quickly, knowing that if the US government could cover up the shuttle disaster, they could track her.

What if Creed knew about Alicia? Would he hurt her? Sandra, for the first time, let her emotions be shown. She took a seat near the bar and started to cry. Why was this happening to her and Alicia? What did Alicia know or see, if anything? Did she get caught in the clouds? Sandra looked up to find Lazarr was standing over her. "You all right?" she asked.

"Yes, I'm OK. That's it," she said. "That's what had to happen. They got caught in the clouds."

"Who?" Lazarr asked.

Sandra ran into the hotel, jumped into the elevator, and headed back to the suites. Louis was staring into the microscope in disbelief. "Tim, Sandra, come here."

"What is this?" Tim said.

"I'm not exactly sure," he said. Then he asked, "Where's Sandra?"

Neither of them had seen her leave. The door opened, and Sandra walked in. "It was the clouds. They killed my sister's friends out on that boat. It has to be."

"You're almost right," Louis said, "but it's not the clouds, it's what's in the clouds."

CHAPTER 39

Creed and Damon were approaching Tim's house. Instead of pulling them over like Sanchez had instructed, the two officers watched them go to the door. When no one answered, they broke in. Creed and Damon ransacked the house, looking for the shuttle scraps but finding nothing. Then Damon found the address to the villa where the Alexanders had been staying.

"Take a look at this, boss," he said. "They may be at this villa."

Creed was looking out the window. He saw the officers sneaking up to the house. "Quiet. We have company. Go out the back, I'll let them in."

Damon did just that. When the officers knocked on the door, Creed opened it.

"Put your hands up and turn around," one of the officers demanded, both pointing their guns at Creed's head.

"No," Creed said. "I think both of you should drop your weapons and step inside now."

"What?" one of the officers said, and then both felt guns pressed to the backs of their heads.

"Do as the man said. Drop your weapons now."

The officers complied, and then Damon stuck one with a hard blow to the back of the head, which sent him dropping to the floor. "Pick him up," Creed told the other. Creed now was pointing his gun at the officer's head.

"Over there on the couch. So, Sanchez had us followed. Well then, you should be able to answer a few questions for us," he said as he lit his cigar. "If I even think you're lying, my friend here will shoot your partner's eyes out. Now tell me, where are Tim Coles and the girl?" Creed asked while blowing cigar smoke in his face.

"Wait," the officer said, "we were just told to follow you and pull you over if you came to this house. I don't know where they are."

"Damon," Creed said. There were two silent shots, and blood splashed onto the wall. All you could see was two big holes in the officer's head where his eyes used to be. The remaining officer shit and pissed his pants. "Please don't kill me. I have a wife and son at home. I—I don't know where they are, I swear."

Creed slapped him in the mouth with his gun, and the officer spit out two teeth. "Do you want to end up like your dead friend here, boy?"

"No, sir."

Creed hit him again. "OK, then I have another question for you. Damon, show him the address. Who lives here?"

"It's a villa. The owners rent it out this time of year. There's a family from the States there now. Sanchez was there looking for the girl a couple of days ago, I think," the officer said while sobbing and crying.

"Stop crying like a little bitch. You should have pulled us over like your boss told you, because then you'd still be alive." *Bam!* Creed's gun sounded like a cannon. The bullet went straight through the officer's brain. "Throw them in the basement," Creed said as he walked over to the stove and turned on the gas. "Let's go to the villa."

CHAPTER 40

Before relocating to the Marriot, Trish had called Captain Sanchez. She was going to tell them what she knew and take the kids and leave the island with or without her husband. Sanchez was not there when she had called, and she'd left a message for him to meet her at the Seaport Mall in Downtown Aruba at three. There was an ice cream shop, and that's where she said she would be. Everyone was too wrapped up in what they were doing and didn't see her leave. She caught a cab out in front of the hotel and was on her way. Trish had forgotten that Tim warned them to be careful because rain was in the forecast.

Sanchez and Caleb were waiting at the mall when he got a call about a house explosion. Tim Coles's house. He had not heard from the two officers that were following Creed, so this worried him. He tried to reach them. No answer. No one had seen them for hours, nor had they reported back to the station. "Get out to Tim's house, Caleb. I'm going to wait for Mrs. Alexander. She knows something. She's scared and ready to talk. Oh, one more thing, Caleb, keep your radio on, and call me soon as you find out what happened."

"Will do, sir." Caleb got into the squad car and pulled off just when the cab with Trish pulled up. Sanchez saw her get out the cab and waved her over to the table. Trish was wondering if she was doing the right thing, and then she suddenly felt sick. She told Sanchez to excuse her for a second, and then she went to the bathroom and puked. After cleaning herself up, Trish returned from the restroom, pulled up a seat, and began to tell Captain Sanchez what she knew about the twins, her family's involvement, and how they thought it was something in the clouds. She only wanted to get her kids off this island.

"Where is your family now, Mrs. Alexander?" Sanchez demanded. "Is Tim Coles with them?"

CHAPTER 41

"What is it?" Sandra asked.

"Some type of parasite," Louis replied.

"A parasite?" Tim asked.

"Yes, look, these are the scraps from the shuttle. You see the bacteria-looking shapes moving around? They're alive but barely, and they're feeding on the scraps."

"Sandra, didn't NASA say the cause of the shuttle crash was foam?"

"Is this the reason Creed is after this shit? Because of a cover-up?" Louis demanded to know.

Sandra stood silent.

"Look at this." Louis put in a sample from the airplane scraps. "You see, same thing, except three times more of them. These are fresh scraps from the plane. They're still moist."

"I don't follow." Tim said.

"Well, I need to do some more tests, but it looks like they're oxygenating."

"What do you mean?" Sandra asked.

"I can't be sure, and this is a long shot, but if I'm right, we have an enormous problem on our hands."

"Just spit it out," Tim said. "And speak English."

"OK, this is just a theory. A couple of years ago, I read an article about the Mir threat. In that article, a space station was placed in orbit and contracted bacteria and fungi. When the shuttle docked in the space station, these microorganisms attached themselves to it. These organisms, some type of space virus, grew continuously, each generation becoming more aggressive than the last. They covered every corner of the station and demonstrated an appetite for highly durable materials—metals, for instance."

"Hold on," Sandra said. "You're suggesting that there's some type of living virus in the clouds?"

"No, even worse, what we have here is not a virus. These are living, breeding as we speak, parasites. Radioactive parasites."

"Of course," Sandra said. "It wasn't just the seals on the shuttle that broke off and cracked the foam. It was these parasites eating through the vessel, and with radioactive particles on and around the ship, these things have mutated into what you're saying, Louis."

"But what does that have to do with the clouds?" Tim asked.

"I'm not sure yet, but somehow, when the shuttle was coming back into our orbit, these things found new life in the water droplets in the clouds. That's the only way to explain what we have here, and if these things eat through metal, you see the results once they land on human flesh."

"We have to warn the people to stay out of the rain," Sandra said.

"Yes, I agree," Tim said, "but more importantly, we have to find a way to kill them and convince the prime minister to cancel the carnival. Rain is in the forecast."

CHAPTER 42

The fire department was at Tim's house, sorting through the rubble from the explosion. They started finding bits and pieces of what appeared to be human bones and other body parts. Caleb saw the officer's car with no one in it, and then he made his way to the fire chief, who confirmed at least two casualties from the explosion. Caleb called Sanchez and told him the bad news. Sanchez ordered him to find Creed and his man and bring them in, no matter what.

As Caleb was walking back to his car, he noticed a sheet of paper with the address to the villa the Alexanders were staying at and had a feeling that's where Creed and his man would show up next.

*   *   *

Sanchez was waiting for Trish to come back from the ladies' room when Caleb called him. He needed to find out where she and her family were staying. Creed was a danger to them and everyone on the island. Although he didn't quite believe her, he could not look past the fact that people on the island were dying. Something bizarre was happening. He decided he would have to pay Sofie a visit.

Trish was feeling bad about what she had done and was able to sneak away while Sanchez was on the phone. She had not told him where the family was staying. For all he knew, they were still at the villa. She hopped in a cab and headed back to the Marriott.

After a few more minutes of waiting, Sanchez knew she had given him the slip and decided to track down Sofie. He knew where she would be, where she always was—at the Marriott.

CHAPTER 43

Lazarr came in from the pool. She was looking at the news when a breaking story started. It told of the explosion and how they had recovered at least two bodies and were still searching for more. The news then went on to say it was the house of their own weatherman who had not been seen since he took some vacation time off for a couple of days.

"Dad!" she shouted as she approached the back room where her father, Tim, and Sandra were still working.

"Not now, sweetie," he said.

"Yes, Dad, now!" she said in a stronger tone as to command their attention as she put on the TV in that room.

Tim Coles fell to his knees in disbelief. "That's my house! Who would have been at—*no!*" he screamed. Although he and Marie didn't live together, she still had keys and would often just drop by whether he was there or not. "I have to go!" Tim screamed. "My family!"

"Wait, Tim." Sandra blocked him from going out the door. "It's not safe. They didn't say who the victims were, and this looks like Creed's work. Is there anyone you can call to see about your family?"

Marie had told Tim she needed to stop by his house and grab a few things when she left the hotel earlier. *How could I have been so stupid?* he thought to himself. If anything happened to them, their blood would be on his hands. He picked up the phone and was about to call Marie.

"No, Tim, you can't call her. Creed surely knows who you are by now and is looking for you. I'm certain he knows about her too. Where was she going?" Sandra asked.

"To the house," he said. "I have to know."

"OK, call someone who can try and reach her for you."

At that moment, there was a loud knock on the door. Everyone in the room froze and stared at the door. Louis headed for it. He looked into the peephole and then slowly opened the door.

Marie burst into the room in tears, pulling her daughter behind her. "Tim! Where's Tim?"

Tim ran to her, held her, and wouldn't let go.

Sandra went over to Louis. "You need to get the rest of your family up here now. Creed probably has men crawling all over the island by now, and we don't know who he might have gotten to."

"What are you saying?" Louis asked.

"I'm saying get a head count. I don't know if he has linked me and Tim together with you guys."

Then it hit her. She had almost forgotten. "Alicia. I have to get her out of there before he finds her." She needed someone she could trust. It would be too risky to try to get back to Florida now. She wasn't even from there. Who could she—*Sean*, she said to herself. It would have to be him.

CHAPTER 44

The cruise ship named the *Sea Resort* had not yet reached Port Canaveral for the propeller repairs they had called in about, so the harbormaster notified the port's chief executive officer, who called the US Coast Guard to report the ship missing.

CHAPTER 45

The FAA investigators had arrived in Aruba and were questioning Dimo, Stan, and Steve from air traffic control about the condition of the plane and the flight. Tim had not returned the metal samples he'd taken, nor had he called. As far as they knew, he was killed in the explosion. No official word had come out yet on the identity of the remains found at his home.

* * *

Trish was back at the Marriott. The whole family was there when she walked in.

"Where have you been, sweetheart? We were worried," Louis asked.

"I just needed some air, to be alone. Is that OK?" she barked back.

"That's fine, dear," Louis was saying as she walked into one of the bedrooms and slammed the door. "OK, everyone is accounted for, so you guys keep your eyes open when you leave this floor."

"Sure, Dad," Lou Jr. said. "But what are you going to do?"

"I have to get back to work to try and figure this thing out. Tim, I need access to a lab. Sandra, I'm going to need your help."

Sandra was on the phone.

Marie had a brother who worked at the one of the colleges cleaning at night, Tim informed Louis. "That's going to be our best time to travel, with Creed and his men searching for us."

* * *

Lester Creed and Damon had arrived at the Alexanders' villa. They had tied up the staff with the exception of Carl. He also had men on their way to the Crisis Stabilization Center in Fort Lauderdale, where Alicia was. He'd had a hunch Sandra might contact the guard and had a tail on him. Creed began to terrorize the staff while Damon ransacked the place, looking for any clue about the whereabouts of Tim and Sandra.

At first, the staff swore they didn't know anything. Creed told Carl he would shoot them one by one until someone spoke up. No one spoke. Creed stuck his gun in the gardener's mouth and pulled the trigger. The rest of the staff looked on in terror. The women were crying, sobbing. The maid began to choke on her own vomit since her mouth was gagged. Creed let her choke. Her eyes rolled up in her head, and her face turned blue. She died a few seconds later.

Then Carl began to speak. He told them that they had been there and had joined up with the Afro-American family from the States. Creed made him describe each family member. Carl did just that. Damon came down the stairs with a disposable camera that had been left in one of the rooms.

"Look what I found, boss," he held up the camera.

"Good. We'll take it to one of the hour shops to get the film developed. It may have some pictures, but I don't think we'll really need them. How many nigger families of nine could be on the island at once? No matter, Carl here was just about to tell us where they went, but I think he needs a little encouragement. Look in the back, bring that gasoline can I saw in here. We're going to cook the cook!"

Creed smirked as he pulled out a cigar. He took his gun and smacked Carl in the face. Carl fell to his knees. "I think they went—"

Creed kicked him in the face. "Don't want you to think. Want you to be sure, and maybe I'll let you and laundry lady live."

Damon was back now. You could smell the gasoline he'd poured all over the villa. He was now pouring it all over the cook, who was crying and choking from the gas.

"The Marriott!" Carl screamed. "The Marriott!"

Lester pulled out a match, lit his cigar, and threw the match on the cook. He lit up like the flames of a rocket on its way into space. Creed shot Carl in both knees.

"What about her?" Damon asked.

"Let her burn with him." They left her tied in the chair. Carl was on the floor. The cook was done. The rest of the villa was starting to catch fire.

Creed and Damon left the burning villa and headed for the Marriott.

Caleb was about five minutes away from the villa when he saw smoke in the air. Then the sound of sirens. He pulled over as fire trucks whizzed by him. He had a bad feeling in his gut. He prepared himself for the worst. His gut feeling was right. It was the villa the Alexanders were staying in. Was this coincidence? What was going on? Who or what was behind all this? He got out of his car and watched as the firemen attempted to bring the blaze under control. A crowd had gathered. He started helping the firemen with crowd control. Thirty minutes later, the fire was now just smoldering. The firemen found two badly burned, injured people and were working on them by the pool. Caleb wanted to know what they knew, but they were rushed to the hospital. He went to the fire chief to see if there was anything he could share about the situation.

CHAPTER 46

The skies were clear as Tim looked out from the balcony. He needed to get access to the news station on the upcoming weather systems, but that was not going to work. He would just have to watch on the TV for now. The carnival was due to start tomorrow, and all of Aruba would take to the streets. They had to get to the governor and cancel all events, or hundreds of thousands could be killed or injured. He was happy that Marie and his daughter were safe but wondered about his dog. He also wondered who was killed in the explosion. Tim knew he was not going to be able to wait until nightfall. Too many things were happening. And then news came about the fire at the villa.

*   *   *

The US Coast Guard was searching the for the cruise ship. They'd notified the Aruba harbormaster and had two search and rescue boats along with two choppers looking for the ship. Aruba officials were putting together their own search operation. The governor was notified and called a special meeting with the island's prime minister, minister of tourism and transportation (Sofie Labridge), and Captain Sanchez. Sanchez was walking up to one of the hotel clerks to have her page Sofie when his cell phone rang.

Little George, Sugar, and Brie were coming out of a gift shop and headed right for Sanchez. They were about to come into his direct view when the clerk spoke. Sanchez dropped his cell phone. As he bent down to pick it up, they walked right by him.

"I'm not getting an answer," the clerk told him. He signaled for her to hold on while he answered the call. He would have to get back to the Marriot. Now, he was headed for the governor's office when he got the call from Caleb about the fire at the villa and possible homicides. The governor would have to wait.

He headed to the hospital to meet Caleb and hopefully question the two survivors. There had been no word on the whereabouts of Creed and his man. This made Sanchez feel uneasy. What if there was some truth to what Mrs. Alexander told him?

Little George and Sugar never noticed Sanchez in the lobby and proceeded for the pool.

CHAPTER 47

Sandra had been trying to get in touch with Alicia's doctor to no avail. She felt as if her sister was reaching out to her. "I'll be back," she told the others.

"Where are you going?" Tim asked.

"We need new phones, something not linked to any of us. We have to move around. We can't stay here too long. I have a bad feeling. Tim, come with me. Louis, get out of here for a minute. Enjoy the day. We have a lot to do tonight."

Both agreed. Tim didn't mention the fire at the villa. He wasn't quite sure what had happened and didn't want to rattle the Alexanders. They would be safe for now, he thought to himself. He still needed to get to the news station. Then it hit him. He could check on the week's forecast from the airport. It would be easier. She was right, they needed some untraceable phones so they could keep in contact while on the lookout for Creed and his men. They bought five phones in all.

Sandra called Sean. He was almost there. She knew she couldn't keep him on the phone long, fearing Creed would be tracking his calls. Sean promised to get Alicia out of the hospital. He would call her later. Just as he was getting out of his car, he noticed two men stalking him. It was too late now. He had to move swiftly. He had led them right to her.

Alicia was doing much better, although she still wasn't talking. Her color had come back, and she was eating again. She also was having brief flashbacks of the images and blood from the boat. Although she could speak, she hadn't. She needed a way out of this place. Alicia wondered why Sandra had not made contact. Was she OK? How had she gotten back to the States? She was scared but had to stay calm so they didn't overmedicate her.

The security at the Trauma Center was light. Sean was able to schmooze the front desk clerk for information to Alicia's whereabouts. He ducked around the corner and peeked around the wall. They were coming. He hopped in the elevator, pushed the 4th floor button, got out, and ran down the stairs to the second floor. Alicia's floor. Creed's men took the next elevator to four. There was no one around Alicia's room. Sean went in and told her he was a friend of Sandra's. "We have to leave now. They're right behind me."

Alicia slipped on her jeans and top. Sean peeked out the door. Creed's men knew he'd given them the slip and were on their way back down. Sean spotted a delivery-only door. He and Alicia rushed down to the lower level. How was he going to get to his car past the goons? Creed's men were in the lobby questioning the clerk when the alarm went off. It came from the second floor. Alicia's doctor had sounded it when he discovered she was not in her room and her clothes were gone.

"Let's go." Creed's men left for the parking lot. Sean's car was still there. He had spotted a laundry service truck, so he and Alicia hid in one of the dirty laundry bins while the driver was making a drop-off. The driver returned just minutes before the alarm sounded. He was pulling out of the parking lot. They had gotten away for now. Sean called Sandra. "I've got her," he whispered. "Can't talk now."

Creed's men also made a call. "You were right, sir. Ms. Blake's sister was here. The guard got to her before we could. We lost them."

"Get the satellite search set up and GPS tracking on that guard's phone. *Find him, kill him, and bring me the girl!* Fools! Get me a drink!" Creed yelled at Damon. He sat at one of the poolside bars at the Marriott and opened the package from the one-hour photo shop.

CHAPTER 48

Sofie had been in a board meeting when she was summoned to the governor's office. She replied by text, saying she was on her way. Neither the US Coast Guard nor the Aruba search and rescue teams had turned up anything. They planned on searching through the rest of the night. It was a glum outlook. Cruise ships that size don't just vanish. Nevertheless, there were no signs of the ship or the crew.

Sofie had just arrived. The prime minister, harbormaster, and a few members from the council of ministers were all waiting and wondering what this special meeting was all about. Sanchez was a no-show. He left word he would check with the governor later. Sofie was irritated. The carnival was starting tomorrow. Several flights were due in today. Hundreds of people would be checking into the Marriott and all the other hotels. She needed to be there. Finally, Gov. Dirk Staten walked in. Everyone stood.

"Please be seated." He painted a grim outlook. Ships in that area had gone down in the old days, never to be recovered. He assured everyone that his office was keeping a tight watch on everything. He also informed them he had received hundreds of calls from Arubans wanting to know what happened at the beach and at the school. "These things are under investigation, and there is no need for panic. I'm assuming there is a good explanation for all this. Sofie, I need you to express our hospitality to the passengers that were aboard the ship and find rooms for them all. Four to a room. We don't want to lose out on too much revenue. Give them food vouchers for a day. There should be another ship on its way to get them."

"I totally agree, Mr. Governor. We don't want to stir up a panic or rumors. Maybe you should go public and assure the people everything is all right. You want the tourists out spending," Sofie suggested.

*   *   *

It was a beautiful day in Aruba. The skies were clear, the beaches were full, and final preparations were being made for the week-long carnival. With all that had happened, Louis had almost forgotten he and his family were on vacation. He decided to go for a walk and a swim on the beach. Trish settled down too. She was on the balcony. She could see Lou Jr. and Lazarr even from where she was high above them. It was a beautiful view. She poured herself a piña colada, lay back in the lounge chair, and pulled out her book, *Squirrels the Mutation* by Hank Patterson—a horror/thriller that was getting a lot of buzz.

Lethia and Big George were downtown at the mall shopping. The cruise ships were lined up, docking into port. Even the inspectors from the FAA took off early to enjoy this beautiful day. Lethia was buying a gold bracelet when the saleswoman asked where she was from and where she was staying. Lethia was a little suspicious, but she'd always been a very friendly person. "Oh, me, my children, their families—"

"Their families?" the woman interrupted. "You're too young."

Lethia chucked. "No, the grandkids are here too. We rented a villa for the week."

"So then, did you see the fire?" the woman asked while handing Lethia her change and receipt.

"Fire? What fire?" Big George asked.

"At one of the villas," the woman replied. "A couple of hours ago. They say some people died in the fire."

"No, we've been down here all morning," Lethia told her. "My question is, why are they gathering all those people in one area at the port? We kind of overheard something was going on while we were having lunch.

"Yes, one of my customers said a cruise ship went for repairs and disappeared. It never came back for them. They have to put them all in rooms."

"Thank you," Lethia told the woman. "Come on, George, let's see what we can find out." They headed across the street for the port.

Chapter 49

Tim called Dimo, who told him everyone thought he was dead from the explosion at his house. "No, it wasn't us, but I need to stay hidden or dead for now," he'd explained. There was a laptop with Doppler radar installed in the software. He needed that and the miniature satellite antenna from the airport weather station newsroom. Tim asked if the FAA boys had found anything.

"Not yet. They seem inexperienced or just don't have a clue of what they're looking for. Hell, they're trying to get to the other side of the island, if you know what I mean."

"Yeah, I know," Tim told him. Dimo instructed Tim to meet him in the visitor's parking lot. Tim couldn't risk being seen. Dimo couldn't risk being seen with Tim and Sandra or the laptop. "I owe you big-time," Tim said as he and Sandra sped away from the airport.

"Now what?" Sandra asked.

"We should stop for a drink, get something to eat. I have something I have to tell you. I don't know if the Alexanders have heard yet."

"Heard what?" Sandra asked.

"Let's get that drink first." Tim headed back toward Downtown Aruba. Sandra was still worried about Alicia. When Sean said he couldn't talk, it concerned her. She didn't want to endanger them by calling. She would have to wait.

There was a nice pizza shop downtown right by the port where you could get great pizza, seafood, and whatever you wanted, so they went there. Tim ordered pizza with the works, a corona, and a margarita. Sandra ordered some Baileys.

"What is it you need to tell me, Tim?"

"It's about the Alexanders' villa. We were right to move them, we were wrong to leave the staff. The villa was burned to the ground earlier today. There are several unidentified dead bodies. This man Creed, you're right, it looks like he'll stop at nothing to get that space shuttle shit back. We have to find a way to stop him. This is a small island. We're going to have to separate into groups and split up."

"My god," Sandra said. "It's true. All the things I've heard about Lester Creed were true. He makes whole families vanish. There was always fire so the victims could never be identified. Now he's after us."

She almost started to cry. She was terrified of Creed now that she knew he would stop at nothing. And what about the police? They still suspected Alicia and herself of the earlier deaths. She felt like a fugitive. She knew she had to stay strong, see this thing through, and get the truth out, whatever that was. Yes, they needed to get to the college lab tonight.

Tim had gone to the men's room. Sandra felt eerie. A hand reached out and grabbed the back of her shoulder. She screamed, jumped, and knocked over the dishes on the table. She turned around just as Tim ran back over to the table.

"Sorry," Big George said. "Didn't mean to scare you. We saw you guys from over there." He was pointing at the ships.

"What do you know about our villa?" Lethia demanded.

"Stay calm," Tim said. "We don't want to bring any more attention to ourselves. C'mon, we have to all get back to the Marriott, but take this." Tim handed Big George one of the five phones they bought. "Meet us there. Our car's not far. I'll call you when we're en route. Hurry."

Tim started driving in the opposite direction from the Marriot.

"Where are you going?" Sandra asked.

"To see a friend. We need to pick up something." Tim called Big George. "Have to swing by the other side of the island. Get everyone together. We'll meet you guys there in about ninety minutes."

Tim made another call. This time, he spoke in one of the island languages. He hung up the phone.

"What was that all about?" Sandra asked.

"You'll see later."

CHAPTER 50

Alicia was still feeling a little dazed from the medication and confused about what was happening, but she trusted Sean. The two of them were now not only being chased by Creed's goons whom they had lost for the moment, but the police would also be looking for them. At the drivers' last stop, they stole a truck.

"We have to dump this truck and get some new wheels and a room to hole up in until I can figure out a way to get back in touch with your sister. It's not safe to use my phone. I'm sure it's being tracked." Having said that, Sean threw the phone out the window.

"Where is she?" Alicia asked.

"In Aruba."

The tears just started flowing as she remembered. Her friends, all her friends were dead. But how, why, what had happened? Then she spoke. "I need to get back to Aruba now."

CHAPTER 51

Sanchez and Caleb were at the hospital. Carl had been stabilized and was in and out of consciousness. The laundress died from smoke inhalation.

"Can we speak to him?" Sanchez asked the doctor.

"He's in really bad shape. I don't recommend it," the doctor said.

"Look, doc, I've got dead bodies all over this island, and Carl here is the only known witness. I insist."

"OK, but only for a moment. He needs his rest."

Sanchez and Caleb entered Carl's room.

* * *

Big George and Lethia had gathered the family, and everyone was waiting for Tim and Sandra to arrive.

The Marriot was huge; neither Creed nor Damon was having any luck spotting the any of the Alexanders they'd seen in the photos or a large group of blacks. There was no Tim or Sandra either. Creed was going to have to bring in more men. At that moment, he looked at a couple across the hallway pushing a cart toward an employee-only elevator in a section of the hotel that was not yet open. It was them. "Tim and Sandra." Creed spoke into his mouthpiece, summoning Damon as he moved toward the two standing at the elevator. The doors opened, they pushed the cart in, and the doors shut. Creed stopped and just stood at the end of the hall. Damon arrived in the next minute.

The two were walking toward the elevator when a voice called out, "Hey, you two, come here, this section is off-limits." The hotel security guard was coming toward them.

Damon was reaching for his gun when Creed stopped him. "Don't be a fool."

"This section is off-limits. It's not yet open for guests," the guard was saying.

Creed looked at the elevator. "Sorry," he said as he watched the floor buttons stop on twenty. "I thought I saw an old friend of mine go this way."

"I doubt it, sir. Like I said, no guests allowed. Only the construction crew is authorized to be in this area."

Creed and Damon turned and walked away. The guard stopped at the end of the hall, where he was stationed to be to keep all non-authorized people from entering the area.

*　　*　　*

The elevator stopped on the twentieth floor. Sandra had an eerie feeling again, as though they were being watched. "Something's wrong," she told Tim. "Did you notice anyone following us?"

"No," Tim replied. He knocked twice on the door and then opened it with his key card. The Alexanders were all there silent, just staring at the two when they entered the room.

CHAPTER 52

Carl was in great pain, barely clinging to life. He described what had happened and told Sanchez and Caleb that the family was at the Marriott.

"Dammit!" Sanchez shouted. "I was just there. Caleb, call Sofie. Find out their room number. Call them. Get over there and get them out. I pray we're not too late."

All Caleb got was Sofie's voice mail.

*   *   *

On the northern side of the island was the lighthouse, a popular tourist stop. There were great views of the island, and the ATVs and Jeep Safaris always met there before going to the back side of the island. There were no beaches there. The sea was too rough—waves up to 20 feet crashed into the rocks continually. The waves had destroyed the Nature Bridge. But it was still a great trip to make, with a nice sea breeze and a few spotty showers.

There were probably about a hundred people heading there for today's excursions. It was a little cloudy on that side of the island, and cloud cover was moving in. No one on the trip knew anything about what had been happening or about the nimbostratus cloud that was approaching with the winds. Nor would anyone live to tell about it. It was happening again—first the rain, and then the screams, and then the shrieks, and then death. It was quick this time. The cloud was much bigger and looked scarier and was still spreading. The rain had stopped for now, and the cloud just hovered on that side of the island. The winds slowed.

CHAPTER 53

Sofie still hadn't returned Caleb's call. She was in a meeting with parade marshals for tomorrow's parade that went around the whole island. Caleb and Captain Sanchez were just getting to the Marriott.

Lester Creed and Damon were approaching the guard who was still standing in the same spot, denying entrance to anyone trying to get to the elevators of the unopened wing where the Alexanders, Tim, and Sandra were hiding out.

Before Tim and Sandra had returned to the hotel, Tim had made a stop in Saint Nicholas at a friend's house and picked up two duffel bags full of weapons he thought they might need for protection against Creed and his men. Trish was horrified once she found out about the fire at the villa. She told them she'd talked to Sanchez and told him about the clouds theory. She told her husband she was leaving and taking the kids, and if he had any sense, he would do the same. Sandra tried to explain that Creed and his men would find them wherever they went.

"We have to end this ourselves, we're in too deep."

Trish called her a bitch and grabbed her kids. She told Louis that if he stayed, there would be nothing back in the States for him to come home to. She went into the next room, bought airline tickets for a flight leaving later that evening, and began packing her and the children's things. Everyone else agreed to stay and see it through, though they were aware of the danger.

*   *   *

Just as Damon was pulling a syringe out of his pocket to inject into the guard, Creed stopped him. He spotted Caleb and Sanchez down the hall at the front desk.

"Wait," he told Damon. "Let's see what they're up to."

The two men went back to the bar and watched.

The desk clerk had no records of the Alexanders being there. Where had Sofie hidden them, and had Creed and his man gotten there first? Sanchez was visibly upset.

Louis understood some of the reasons his wife was upset, and maybe it was best if she took the kids. Then he thought no, that was the worst thing she could do. If she separated the family, he couldn't protect them. He went back and begged Trish to stay, but she would not listen. He hugged his kids and told them everything would be all right and he would be home soon. His son did not want to leave his father, but his mother demanded he leave with her.

Sofie had told them not to use the lobby elevators and to use the service elevators. Tim and Sandra had ignored that fact. They had realized it once they were in the elevator, so they had pushed the twentieth floor, gotten off, and then taken the service elevators to the twenty-fourth, where the suites were. You couldn't even get there from the other elevators. Trish grabbed her luggage, told Lou Jr. and Lazarr to grab their stuff and get going. Louis went to stop her, but his mother stopped him.

"They'll be all right," she assured him. He watched as the door slammed shut and poured himself a drink.

Big George went after them and gave Trish the phone he had gotten from Tim. "Let us know you're all right."

She thanked him, gave him a hug, got in the service elevator, and left.

CHAPTER 54

Creed and Damon were watching the elevator when the doors slid open. The guard had moved away. He was in a little shop nearby talking to one of the ladies that worked there. Sanchez and Caleb also saw Trish and the kids get out.

They walked out the hotel and got into a cab. Trish told the driver to take them to the airport.

The cops tried to catch the cab but were too late. The vehicle pulled off as they were running behind. Sanchez said, "Get the car, Caleb. Hurry, stop them, don't let them get away."

Caleb went for the car. "What about you?" he shouted back to Sanchez.

"I'm going to find the others."

Creed told Damon, "Follow them and bring them to me."

"What about the cop?" Damon said.

"Call some of the men, head him off. A nice traffic accident should do the trick."

Damon left in pursuit. Creed stood by.

Sanchez was on his way to the elevator when his phone rang. It was Sofie.

"Where are they?" he demanded. "I know they're here in the hotel. Their lives are in danger. Tell me now."

"Who?" Sofie said. "Who is in danger?"

"Tim Coles and the rest of them, dammit." Sanchez was headed for the elevator when the guard stepped back up. He pulled out his badge. "Move aside. Police business."

Both men had their backs turned and didn't see Creed walk up. He stuck a needle in the guard's buttocks. As the elevator was opening, he hit Sanchez in the back of the head with his gun and pushed him on the floor. He grabbed Sanchez's phone. "Where are they?"

Sofie thought it was still Sanchez and told him how to get to the twenty-fourth floor. Creed dragged the guard into the elevator. He was out instantly from the drug. He would die soon, and it would look like a heart attack.

Damon was following Caleb, who was gaining on the cab and was just about to turn his siren on to pull them over when out of nowhere, he was struck hard on his passenger door by a vehicle that had just run the light. He hit his head on the driver's side glass as the car came to an abrupt stop. Two men got out of the car that hit him and headed toward him.

Lou Jr. heard the accident and turned around. "Did you see that? Someone just hit that police car. We should stop and see if they need help."

"No, keep going. Someone else will help them. See those people getting out? They will help," his mother said.

Damon pulled up beside the cab and motioned for them to stop. They did not, so he pulled in front of the cab and slammed on his brakes. They stopped.

"What's going on?" Lazarr was saying as Damon got out. He pulled out his gun, went over to the driver, and shot him twice in the chest. He had a silencer on his gun, so it didn't make a lot of noise. Trish, Lou Jr., and Lazarr were all screaming. "Shut up or you're next. Everyone out now."

CHAPTER 55

Big George had seen Caleb and Sanchez chasing after the cab. He called upstairs to Louis to tell him they had been found and that he had seen Creed hit Sanchez in the head and force him into the elevator. "Get everyone out now," he told him.

Sandra was in the hallway with Tim on the phone. She'd gotten the call from Sean that she'd been waiting on.

Tim was on the phone with Dimo. They had come up with a plan to get Alicia back into Aruba. She wasn't safe in Florida. Dimo would smuggle her in tonight. He knew Stan would be flying the last flight into the island tonight and would be glad to help. They all had a stake in this thing now.

Sean knew he couldn't return to his job and wanted to help, but Sandra said it was too dangerous and didn't want his blood on her hands if anything went wrong. He'd done enough. She told him where to find some cash at her condo and to get as far away from Florida as possible. She would look him up when things were safe, if they made it. Lester Creed was a very dangerous man and had a green light to kill anyone whom he and his peers deemed a threat.

Louis tried reaching his family but got no answer. He and his brother got their mother, their daughter, and Sugar out by way of the back stairway.

Tim and Sandra stayed. They would confront Creed when he got there. They too had armed themselves, and Creed wouldn't dare kill them at this point, as he would need to retrieve the shuttle scraps and find out who else knew about what was going on so he could eliminate all loose ends. This, Sandra was sure about. She was shaking, terrified of what was about to happen when the knock on the door came and the door slowly crept open.

It was Big George. He was hurt. Tim had his gun ready. Sandra stayed out of view with her gun pointed in that direction. Tim grabbed George, and out of nowhere, Creed appeared behind him. Sanchez pointed his gun at Tim and told him to drop his gun.

"Is there anyone else in the room?" he shouted as he pushed Creed onto the floor and grabbed the back of his head.

Sandra came from behind the door and shouted to Sanchez, "No, you drop your weapon now!"

Sanchez turned and pointed his gun at her. "Look, lady, I'm the law on this island. I'm here to help," he said, pointing his gun back at Creed and putting him in the chair. "Tend to your friend. He's been hurt badly."

Tim put Creed in a chair after Sanchez had managed to cuff him. "Tie him up with something!" Sanchez shouted as he fell to the floor himself.

CHAPTER 56

Damon had taken Trish and the kids back to his and Creed's since there was no answer when he tried to call Creed to let him know he had intercepted his target. He had them bound and gagged in a locked room in the dark.

Creed's men had shot Caleb twice in the chest and put him in the trunk.

CHAPTER 57

The passengers from the ship that was now being reported as missing were put up in the first ten floors of the closed wing at the Marriott, a task Sofie took on herself. Those floors were ready, but the higher floors still had a few minor touches to be finished. She would charge the cruise line for the rooms. She had meant to call Tim and warn him that Sanchez was on to them but had entirely forgotten when she could not find the guard and had to place everyone in rooms herself with the help of a newly hired hotel clerk. She was still inquiring what had happened to the guard who was supposed to be watching the area while she personally saw to it that everyone was accounted for.

At the police station, the phones were ringing off the hook from tourists calling about their loved ones who hadn't returned from the tour to the other side of the island. Some of the tour operators had been calling too when their buses did not return on schedule. One of the police clerks from the station had been trying to reach Sanchez and Caleb but was not getting anywhere and didn't know what to tell any of the callers, so she decided to call the governor's office.

Dirk Staten was also being bombarded with calls about the missing cruise ship, missing tourists, and what had happened at the beach and school. He and the other ministers, with Sofie on conference call, were in a meeting and issued a gag order to the police, the cruise line, the news, and the papers while everything was still being investigated, so as to not alarm the public about the events of the last few days. It meant too much revenue to the island to not have the streets filled and people spending. The carnival was set to kick off officially tomorrow, although the locals would start with the street pajama party parade and a concert in Saint Nicholas tonight.

*   *   *

"Next, the forecast for all you pajama partiers tonight and a forecast for the beginning of carnival week. Looks like some scattered showers heading our way. When we come back. I'm Natasha Stevie for *News Now*, Aruba's ten-o-clock news."

Everyone at the news station was still in disbelief about the news of Tim and his family's apparent tragic deaths from the fire, although the bodies had not yet been identified.

*   *   *

Stan has safely gotten Alicia to Aruba and met up with Dimo, who told her he would take her to a woman named Marie and that she would explain everything to her and take her to her sister. Alicia was feeling much better now, but she could not get those images out of her head. *What had happened while I was in the water?* she kept pondering as the car sped down the highway. He stopped at a Valero gas station a few miles later. Marie was waiting. As Alicia sat there, she felt a feeling of danger. *Could I trust these people?* she thought to herself as Dimo opened her door.

"Come on, we don't have a lot of time. I have to get back to work before anyone misses me."

Alicia hesitated, and then she spotted a little girl asleep in the backseat of the car Dimo was leading her to, so that was comforting. Hell, for all she knew, they could be responsible for what happened on the *Two of Us. Get it together, girl,* she told herself. Why bring a kid if something was up? Dimo opened the passenger's door, and Alicia got in.

"Hi, I'm Marie, and that's my daughter Tania in the back."

Alicia could see the child had some bandages on her arm. Then she spoke. "I'm Alicia Blake. Where is my sister?"

Dimo tapped on the hood twice, and Marie pulled off. "I'm going to take you to her now," she said as she pulled out of the gas station. "I'll explain everything I know on the way."

*   *   *

Caleb woke up in what appeared to be the trunk of a car. He could barely make out what two men were talking about. He was thankful he had worn his vest today. It was a new one—very thin, a prototype he'd borrowed from the station. But there was blood on his shirt. One of the bullets had penetrated the vest. He was in pain and must have passed out from being shot at close range, but he was still alive and thankful for that. The two goons probably thought he was dead, but what were they planning to do with him? The smell of the sea was strong, and he could now hear the sounds of the waves crashing against the rocks. They were planning on dumping him in the sea, that had to be it, he figured as the car came to a stop.

CHAPTER 58

Creed's phone rang. Tim and Sandra both looked at him.

"What do we do?" Tim asked.

"It's probably one of his goons. We need to find out what he wants and where they are. They could be here in the hotel right behind him. We have to get him out of here," Sandra replied.

"But George is hurt badly." He was beaten badly in the struggle in the elevator. He was stabbed in the back, had two broken ribs, and a broken arm. "We need to get him to the hospital now."

Creed had done this to the elderly man. Big George had gotten into the elevator just as it was closing. Creed was about to kill him when Sanchez finally woke up and was able to get hold of his weapon which was lying on the floor. The guard was dead.

"Answer it," Sanchez muttered, "Put it on speaker and up to his mouth." He pointed at Creed as he got himself off the floor.

"One wrong word, and you're dead," Sanchez said to Creed as he slapped him in the face. "One fucking word." He had his gun to the back of Creed's head."

"Damon," Creed said.

"Yes, boss, it's me. You OK? I've called a few times."

"I'm good. Did you get the package?" he smirked as he asked.

"Got them right here, boss."

Who? Tim and Sandra wondered.

"There's a bit of a problem," Creed said. "I'm here with—"

Sanchez put his gun on Creed's temple to warn him.

"Who is 'them'?" Sandra whispered for Creed to ask.

"Who?" Creed asked.

"I have the wife and the two kids. The cop is being disposed of as we speak. What problem, boss?"

Sanchez snatched the phone. "This is Captain Sanchez," he shouted, "and if you lay a hand on any one of those people, I'll blow your boss's brains out of his skull right now! Where are you, and where are you holding them?"

"Hang up!" Creed shouted. Damon did just that. Sanchez punched him in the face.

"Stop it," Tim said. "We're going to need him alive. Gonna have to make a trade for the family."

Sanchez slapped him one more time, put the gun to his head, and told him, "You're a dead man, mister. It's just a matter of time."

Then he said to Tim and Sandra, "You two come over here."

"We've got to get him some help," Sandra said as she tried to comfort Big George, "or he's not going to make it."

"Tim, call Sofie. Have her make sure this area stays secure, and I'll get him a police escort to the hospital and put some men there to watch him and keep him safe. Brave old fuck risked his life for all of us. Now tell me exactly what the shit is going on here. My friend may have died because of it. *All of it, now!*" Sanchez demanded.

*   *   *

It had been hours since Louis, his brother, Sugar, Brie, and their mother had heard anything from anyone else in the family. They were all a bit frantic. Why hadn't his wife at least called to say they were all right? And why wouldn't she answer? They all had the phones that had been given to them. Big George had gone to give her one, and now he too wasn't picking up. They were sitting in a bar on the pier of the beach, just waiting.

"Something's wrong. We have to go back," Louis was saying.

"Look, I know how you feel, bro. We all feel the same. Something is off, but we can't go back there. We have to give it a little more time. We need to just sit tight a little longer."

At that moment, Louis's phone rang. It was Tim. "What's up?"

He got very quiet as his whole demeanor changed.

"What's wrong?" his mother asked. "What is it?"

Louis gave the phone to his brother. Tim told him what had happened and told him about his father who was barely hanging on.

"Mom," Little George said, "you and Sugar need to go to the hospital. Dad's been hurt. Bro, I need you to get it together. We've got to go now, and I mean now. You know what's at stake. This whole thing's blowing up right in our face, and there ain't gonna be nobody left to tell about it. The clouds are moving in fast, not to mention—"

Louis cut him off. "I know." He leaned over and gave his mom a kiss. "We love you, Mom. Get to the hospital."

George gave his wife and daughter a kiss. Brie, who was only nine, seemed oblivious to all that was happening. She was preoccupied with her phone. Louis and his brother walked across the sand to the parking lot, got into the car, and sped off toward the lab at the college with George behind the wheel. Lethia, Sugar, and Brie took a cab to the hospital.

CHAPTER 59

Tim, Sandra, and Sanchez—with Creed in tow—were headed for the pajama parade in Saint Nicholas. They had determined that would be the best place to make the trade. Lester Creed for Louis's wife and kids. It would be packed and very well lit, although they knew Damon would have men there. Tim had put in a call to his friends on the island. They would serve as muscle to make sure nothing happens during the exchange.

Sanchez couldn't get the police involved. He needed all his men he could to get people inside the bars in case the burning rain came—or parasites, as Tim and Sandra had tried to explain to him, which he was having a hard time believing. He needed proof, but he didn't want it in the way of more dead bodies. Tim checked the forecast and told Sanchez the partiers were in danger if it was a nimbostratus cloud.

CHAPTER 60

The trunk of the car opened, and two shots were fired. Creed's goons fell to the ground, shot dead. Caleb dragged himself out of the trunk and into the driver's seat. He was hurting badly, but he knew he had to push on. He'd grabbed a phone from one of the dead bodies and made the call to Sanchez. Sanchez was elated that his lieutenant was still alive. He didn't want Creed to overhear this, so he texted Caleb about what was happening and told him to get to the hospital, which Caleb refused to do, instead opting to go to the lab to meet up with Louis and George to see if there was any truth to this wild story about what was happening on the island and find out how to stop it.

* * *

Alicia Blake, like her twin sister, was a beautiful, educated woman. She was a top dive master and had logged over two hundred dives around the world. She was one of the most sought-after divers in the States for tourists seeking adventure and salvaging companies looking for treasure. She possessed an eighth degree black belt, which came in handy when going up against some of the shady crews seeking riches at any cost for sunken treasure. She owned her own tourist business and occasionally would take classified jobs from the United States government to retrieve space junk that had fallen into the oceans and seas. Alicia also was an underwater explosives expert, which came in handy for the many cover-ups or when there was a need to destroy top secret military objects lost at sea that had gone irretrievable.

She now was speeding down a highway to meet up with her sister who had come to the island looking to protect her, although she didn't need it. A family from the States, whom her sister had become involved with, were now in one of the biggest cover-ups in the history of space exploration. She had purposely bought her friends to the island and signed on with NASA after learning about her sister's work one night while the two were tipsy after a couple of bottles of wine. Sandra wasn't supposed to be here. None of this should have ever happened, but while looking for parts of the shuttle, the technicians had miscalculated where some of the scraps from the explosion had landed until a salvaging ship searching for treasure mistakenly found some of the pieces in the Caribbean Sea. Her cover was just that of a tourist guide. No one knew. Now she knew that she had been lied to and the real danger everyone was in. There was a real danger to the people on the island, to herself, and to her sister, and it might just cost them their lives.

Alicia had been suffering from blackouts for about a year now because of the deep depths of her dives and the aftershocks of some of the close calls from the explosives she had used. This, along with the head blow from Najee, was what sent her into a state of shock. It had worn off completely now, and she was fine.

"Here we are," Marie said as she pulled up to the lab. "They're going to meet us here. The others are inside."

Alicia, Marie, and Tania all went inside the college. Little George was waiting for them. Louis had taken the metal scraps from the hotel and was running tests on the radioactive parasites. He pondered how this came to be. He was also worried about his family. He hoped everything would go well with the trade—Creed for his loved ones. He wanted to be there, but he knew he was needed at the lab to try and find a way to defuse or kill the parasites before more people got killed.

But he needed to know exactly what was going on, and he had suspicions about the twins. Sandra knew more than she had told him. Being a biochemist was not a very popular field where he'd come from (Detroit), but he had always been fascinated with science. His long hours at work, his and his wife's continuing education, the kids—it had all taken its toll on his marriage. This trip was supposed to be a last attempt to save their marriage. After what had occurred here on the island, he knew if he got his family back alive and off the island, that would be it.

He looked up at Alicia. She was beautiful, just like her twin sister. He strangely felt some sort of vibe between him and Sandra, or was he just lusting? It had been nearly a year since he and his wife had been intimate, and he ached to hold women in his arms.

His brother walked over to him. "You OK? What do you see?"

Alicia too was standing next to George.

"Take a look, both of you." He got up, and one after the other, they peered into the microscope.

"So what does it mean?" Alicia asked. "And where's my sister?"

Louis looked around the room. He found a lab rat, grabbed its cage, and bought it over to the table. He then took a knife, put some water on it, and sat it on the metal from the shuttle. Alicia and George looked puzzled.

"OK, bro, what are you doing? You going to cut the rat?"

"No," he said. "Even worse. Come over here." He motioned to the two of them. Tania was asleep, and Marie had also come over to the table everyone was now standing at. There was a much bigger microscope on it. Louis took the cage with the rat in it and placed it under the microscope. Then he grabbed the knife, being very careful about where he grabbed it.

Just when it seemed to the others that he was going to cut the rat with the knife, there was another knock on the door. The four of them looked at one another. Alicia went and stood behind the door. "See who it is," she said to Marie.

Louis hoped it was the others with his wife and kids. Marie slowly opened the door. On the outside was a man on the ground. It was Lieutenant Caleb.

"It's the lieutenant!" Marie shouted. "He's hurt, help me get him in here quick."

Alicia and George helped with the lieutenant. Louis sat the knife down. "Is he OK?"

"Nope," his brother answered. "Looks like he's been shot."

"Lay him down on this table over here," Marie said. "Look for some first aid kits and get me some fresh water and towels. He's lost a lot of blood."

Caleb had taken the vest off while driving, and in doing so, the bullet wound opened.

"Go to my car," Marie said. "There are some liquor bottles in the trunk. Get them and bring them here."

"OK," Alicia said. "You come with me." She grabbed George.

"Wait, get his keys. Move that car away from here. We don't know if whoever did this to him is on his tail. Move both cars across the street. It's starting to look suspicious, and we're not supposed to be here," Marie said.

"Will do, lady," George replied. As the two were coming back across the street, they didn't notice the shadowy figure watching them as they reentered the school. The man watching them was on the phone. He was told by Damon to stay put. Creed would want to know their location.

CHAPTER 61

"The rest of our forecast looks like spotty showers tonight and low-level clouds moving in, making their way all around the island for the rest of the week. This will cause heavy downpours at times, but they shouldn't last too long, so for all you partiers, and this means the whole island, just be prepared to get a little wet at times. The highs will continue into the upper eighties with those trade winds moving the clouds at times and low precipitation. So it looks like the rain clouds are here to stay. I'm Natasha Stevie, and this has been your *Weather Now* forecast."

The station's producer went to commercial break.

"What the hell is going on?" Natasha said. "We're getting hundreds of calls about there possibly being some type of chemical spraying going on under our noses, hundreds of people injured, if not dead, and we have a gag order not to report it from the governor, Tim wouldn't stand for this if he were here. Our job is to report the news, the facts."

"Well, Natasha, that's the problem. We don't have all the facts now, do we?"

"This is bullshit, and you know it!" she shouted. "I'm going to find out exactly what's going on. I'll get you your facts."

"Just be here in the morning to cover the morning weather," the producer said as she walked out the door.

Chapter 62

The streets were full as Tim pulled over. "We have to walk from here." There was loud music, marching bands, and thousands of people who had converged on Saint Nicholas for the pajama party and concert tonight. The local hookers had even shut down shop for tonight. Aruba's own Caribbean Kings were set to perform. They had the number one song in the islands and were even getting some airplay in the States. Creed was still handcuffed as Sanchez dragged him out of the car. Sandra was nervous, hand on weapon. Tim got on his phone. On the other end, a voice was saying everyone was in place, and there were definitely some strange characters lurking about.

Damon had Trish and the kids standing on a corner. They each had a goon holding on to them at gunpoint. He'd told them if any one of them did anything out of the ordinary, he would have them killed. Louis Jr. spotted Tim. He was talking on the phone with Damon.

"OK, send them now. We'll bring your man across to you. Oh, and look around you. Anything goes wrong, my people will shoot you and your men dead," Tim said.

Damon looked around him and surveyed the crowd. One man with a red bandana showed his weapon and winked at him. Damon took another look. There were several people in the crowd with those red bandanas on, all focused on him and his men. He growled to himself and spoke into his headpiece. "Stand down, everyone."

He released Trish and the kids. They made their way across the street as Sanchez moved slowly toward Damon with Creed still in cuffs. Sandra grabbed Lou Jr. and told Trish and Lazarr to come with her quickly.

Trish said, "Get your hands off my child, you bitch."

"Bitch," Sandra said.

"Not now, ladies. We have to get out of here," Tim said, stepping in between them.

Sanchez whispered into Creed's ear, "You're a dead man, sir."

Creed smiled, turned around, and watched as Sanchez slowly backed away. Then there was a loud boom. It was the sound of thunder. The clouds had moved in. No one had paid attention to this while they were making the trade. The rain started. Nothing was happening. It was a slow tickle, and then there was more thunder. Lightning lit up the sky. The people in the crowd were all staring up at the clouds. When the lightning lit up the sky, you could see something in the clouds, but what was it? It gave the appearance of hundreds of thousands of fireflies, blue and green lights coming from them and descending down upon the crowds.

Then the screaming started. There was chaos, panic, and death. Sanchez gave the order to his officers, and at once they were trying to move people into the bars and stores. Tim, Sandra, Lazarr, Lou Jr., and Sanchez had all ducked inside a bar. Lou Jr. was staring at one of the night ladies who just winked at him.

Creed, Damon, and their men had gotten inside too. "What's happening?" Creed demanded to know.

"Not sure," Damon said.

"Give me your phone now!" Creed shouted. "And get these fucking cuffs off me."

"Yes, sir."

"Don't let anyone else in here."

"But what about those people out there? They're dying." Damon acted like he had a soft spot. "Do you wish to join them, Damon? Would you like to give them your spot? Give me that phone now."

Lester Creed was embarrassed about being captured and held hostage by mere civilians. He'd made a mistake, and he knew he should have taken Tim and Sandra at the space station when he'd had the chance. Now he was going to make them pay, all of them, their families. Now he would have to get to the governor to downplay what was happening. Although he wasn't quite sure what it was, he knew it was on NASA.

The rain had come to an end. Tim, Sandra, Trish, and the kids were in the car headed for the college. He'd called ahead to tell Louis his family was safe. Louis had spoken to his son. His wife refused to speak with him; she just wanted off the island. She felt deep down that there was something going on between her husband and that woman who, as far as she was concerned, had caused all this. She thought, *Fuck him. This bitch could have him.* She had taken out a large insurance policy on him a while back, when he was drinking heavily. It was just a matter of time before he drank himself to death or ended up in jail.

He had helped raise the kids, but the time had come for her to move on. He didn't love her, or her him. They were basically just there for the kids. She'd gotten pregnant early on when they were dating and had threatened to take his only son if he didn't marry her, so he'd agreed to that. But Louis had his share of issues too. He was once a drug dealer. Because of his knowledge in chemistry, he'd been approached at a young age to mix things and sell them. It helped get her and Lazarr out of their decaying neighborhood and later on bought them a nice house in the suburbs.

There were no two rights or wrongs about it, they were both guilty. They both loved their kids, but their time had come. This was just the straw that broke her back. No more. She had to get off the island at any cost. She had tried to cut a deal with Damon to spare her life and that of her children. She'd told him about what her husband and the others thought was in the clouds.

He figured it was just a desperate attempt to spare her, but now he knew there was some truth to her story based on what he had just witnessed. He needed to tell Creed what he knew. Creed was behind the bar pouring himself a drink while he was in deep conversation with his boss, Luther Page, the director of NASA.

CHAPTER 63

Luther Page told Creed that he needed to get the space shuttle scraps back to the space center immediately and dispose of the Alexanders and everyone else involved, especially Alicia Blake and her sister. He told Creed that he need not be worried about the law there. Everything was under control, meaning a cover-up was already in place. The United States would deny any and everything. The blame would be shifted to neighboring Venezuela and Cuba.

Dirk Staten, the governor, and the rest of Aruba's ministers had been paid off by western corporations and government officials back in the nineties. Some of the officials back then had succumbed to pressure or had mysteriously vanished altogether (sudden death syndrome), leaving the little island whose remaining officials had at once vowed to stop building any more hotels after the Marriott. Aruba was now a hot spot, and American as well as European tourists were flocking there year-round to get in on the excitement as well as the easy startup business or real estate.

Creed knew not to ask for more details. He was a goon, a hired killer who enjoyed killing for whatever the reason. They paid him well, and that was all he needed to know.

"Damon, come over here," Creed said as he poured himself another drink and one for Damon. "Tell me what you know about our little friends here on the island and the States. Don't leave out anything."

Damon told Creed he knew where they were holed up. It had just been confirmed that the others had arrived at the college.

"Good, keep our man out of sight and get a couple more guys over there in case anyone leaves. I want to know where all of them are from this point on and what they're doing. I need eyes and ears in that place now. Also, get the rest of the men. We're going over there. We're going to put an end to this bullshit. Now," Creed barked as he slammed his glass and poured yet another.

"I think I know how we can find out exactly what they're planning and doing, sir. The wife wants to make a deal. She's willing to give them all up for safe passage off the island for her and her kids."

"That's great. We'll bite. Tell her whatever she needs to hear. We'll get her off the island and take care of her back in the States. Tell her we'll pay her handsomely for her help." Creed was looking over everyone's personal files which he now had. He saw the insurance policy she had on her husband. "One more thing, Damon. Did we take care of our little security guard back home?"

"Yes, sir," Damon said as he pulled out his phone and showed Creed a picture of Sean in Sandra's condo, lying in a pool of blood with two bullet holes in his chest and one to the head. He had about $10,000 on him and was just about to leave when Creed's men caught him inside her place, shot him, and killed him. They were dressed like police officers checking on an apparent break-in when they caught up with him. No one would question them. Sean was gone. The management at the condo had tried to get in touch with Sandra but had no such luck and had told Creed's men they were unaware of her whereabouts at the time of the incident. Sean's last communication to Sandra was "Got it. See you soon." She assumed he had made it out of the state and was safely in hiding somewhere. Creed's death count was rising.

*   *   *

Big George had been stabilized and put into intensive care. He was barely holding on. There was nothing Lethia and Sugar could do but wait and pray. Sugar sent her husband a text message informing him of his father's condition and to let him know they were OK. She told him the police were there keeping an eye on them, but she felt something was wrong. She had an uneasy feeling about one of the officers who kept texting someone. Her husband told her to make contact with the officer to see if she could get any information out of him. He also told her that everyone was safe and had made it to the college.

What Little George didn't know was that this was no real police officer. It was one of Creed's men, and he had been given the order to kill them all—Sugar, Lethia, Big George, even the kid.

*　*　*

The governor was in his office with Sofie. He had gotten the call from the director of NASA who informed him that his men on the island were to have full jurisdiction over the situation. He'd also lied and told him that the US had been watching Cuba and Venezuela for some time now. They got the blame for deaths on chemical warfare trials aimed at a later attack planned for Florida. Aruba had been chosen because of all the corporations now operating on the island. The director also told them in no way were they to shut down the carnival. Sofie was overjoyed about this. All she ever saw was money. Director Perry told him Lester Creed would be paying him a visit shortly with a little bonus for his cooperation and further directions.

Governor Staten looked at Sofie. "This is wrong. Our people are dying, and for what? A few million dollars? It just isn't right," he said as he poured himself a drink and sat down behind his desk.

Sofie poured herself a drink. "Don't lose your balls now. Do you know how much we stand to make by helping them? You heard what he said. They're gonna pay and take care of everything. Grow some balls, Dirk. Better yet, let me help you with that."

Sofie stood in front of the governor and took off her blouse, exposing her breasts. She then dropped to her knees and unzipped his pants. "Everything is going to be just fine" were the last words he heard as her mouth covered his penis.

CHAPTER 64

Almost everyone was around the table inside the lab, with the exception of Trish, Lazarr, and Tania. Caleb was still out of it. Louis Jr. refused to sit in the corner with his mother and sister. He wanted to see what his father was about to do. Louis had been going over his theory about the parasites. Now, with almost everyone present, he grabbed the lab rat and the knife again. He looked as if he was going to cut the rat.

Sandra shouted, "Stop! What are you doing?"

"Just wait. I'm not going to hurt him, but all of you need to see this." Louis slid the knife over the side of the rat. He was careful to make sure everyone saw that he did not cut the rat himself. He then sat the knife down and invited each of them to look into the microscope at the rat. What they saw turned their stomachs. The rat was being eaten alive by what looked like shining little blue and green lights with razor-like pinheads tearing away at the flesh while going ever deeper into the carcass until there was nothing left.

"What are they?" Tim asked.

"Like I said, my best guess is some type of radioactive parasite," Louis replied. "But Sandra, please feel free to jump in anytime now. I believe you should be able to fill in the blanks."

His comments were not meant to be harsh or accusatory, but everyone needed to know what they were up against. Sandra didn't take it that way either. She could hear the concern in his voice. She also saw the way he looked over to the corner at his wife, and then the soft look he gave her. She was feeling something for this man, but it would have to wait. Everyone's lives on the island depended on it, based from what she just saw and feared to be true. It would explain everything—Creed, the murder of Tim Coles's friend Jason Pitts, and the truth behind the shuttle disaster. Sandra had noticed the box with the liquor in it from Marie's trunk sitting on the desk. She walked over to it as everyone waited for her to speak.

"Some of ya might want to join me because what I'm about to tell you all is classified, and we're all in danger of losing everything we love and hold dear to us."

Louis went over and poured himself a drink. He could see his wife glaring at him from the corner of his eye. He wasn't concerned with that right now, so he went ahead anyway. He also could see she was hiding something. He'd seen her put her cell phone down the side of her leg.

"Yeah, I'm with that," Tim joined in. "It's been a long day." He too poured himself a drink and one for Marie.

Little George joined in. "Why not? Some kinda vacation, huh?"

Alicia moved over to one of the windows.

Sandra began by telling everyone that she was a radiation specialist for NASA and on loan to the space center in Florida from the facility in New Mexico to investigate the shuttle explosion. Director Luther Page had called her in as a subject matter expert on gamma radiation. She explained to them that this was what the blue– and green-looking lights coming off the parasites was.

"This probably was caused by ionizing radiation, which is radiation composed of particles that can by themselves sometimes carry kinetic energy. This was more than likely caused by millions of electrons from an atom or molecule that got generated by nuclear reactions."

"The space shuttle?" Tim blurted.

"I think so, because of the very high temperature, via production of high energy particles caused by an acceleration of gamma-charged particles. That is my belief. As the shuttle passed through electromagnetic fields, anything from lighting to supernova explosions could have caused these space parasites to become active and begin chewing thought the ship."

"What the *fuck* are you talking about?" Little George shouted. "I mean really, what in the *fuck* are you saying? This time in English. Break that science shit down, we're not at NASA."

"Sorry," Sandra said.

"I agree with George. What are you talking about?" Marie jumped in.

"There's something in the rain, some kinda chemical."

"That's what NASA wants everyone to believe," Tim Coles said. "I think I get it now. Jason was on to them, and now, Sandra, you've hit it on the nose. But how did the parasites get in the raindrops? Here's my guess, you two stop me if I'm too far off. This would also explain the metal scraps from the plane being damaged on the flight you all were on coming to the island. If what you say is true, then the space shuttle, while docked at the space station, must have been contaminated with these parasites, right?"

"That's right," Louis said. "My theory is that the ship got contaminated with some type of unknown space bacteria fungus that, because of some type of radioactive decay, allowed them to be exposed to a nuclear transmutation."

Tim jumped back in. "Which, when the shuttle came back into our atmosphere, it must have gone through a nimbostratus cloud full of water droplets. The parasites probably jumped ship and found life in the oxygen in the raindrops, giving them a new home in which to breed, and we know the rest."

Alicia came to the table. "We got a problem. We're being watched. We have to get outta here now."

"Wait, how do we stop this? It's not just going to go away. And if a strong enough wind comes and carries one of these clouds across the water, what then?" George asked.

"Screw across the water. They're the ones who let this happen and now are trying to cover it up by killing all of us," Marie said.

"Listen, folks, we have to go now," Alicia said again. "Everyone get ready. I'm going to get a closer look outside. Pack up whatever we need. We're going to have to split up. We don't have enough transportation for all of us in one vehicle."

Trish came over to the table and said, "This is all the fault of you two. Why can't we just stay here and call for help?"

"Because no help is coming. If we figured all this out, you can bet Creed and the US government know it, so we're all expendable. They don't want us to get this information out there, they are going to kill all of us, I know it," Alicia said. "And someone watch this bitch." She pointed at Trish. "She's up to something. Sandra, I've got something I have to confess to you and everyone in this room, but not now. We have to move."

"I'll come with you," George said.

"Wouldn't have it any other way," Alicia replied as the two headed out the lab and down a dark hallway.

"What's she talking about?" Louis asked his wife.

"Oh, screw you, Louis," Trish said. "This is your last chance to do the right thing by me. Are you with me, us, our family? Or these two bitches? I can help. I can get us out, but not them. Give those men what they want."

"What have you done, Trish? Tell me now." Louis grabbed her arm.

"Get your fucking hands off me now," Trish said, snatching her arm away from him.

CHAPTER 65

The fake police officer at the hospital was ready to make his move. He'd told the real officer to go get them some refreshments. He was just about to enter Big George's room when Sugar came over.

"Hey, what are you doing? Why are you going in there?" she asked.

"Just going to see if he's awake yet. We need to get a statement from him about who did this to him," the fake cop replied.

"OK, I'll come in with you. He's my father-in-law." Sugar didn't see the syringe he stuck back into his pocket as they both entered the room. Lethia and Brie were asleep in the waiting room nearby. There was no one at the nurses' station. Sugar knew there was something wrong. She spotted a vase on one of the tables and moved toward it as the fake cop approached George. He had the syringe in his hand and was just about to inject him when there was a crash upside his head. He fell to the floor and dropped the syringe. Sugar picked it up and injected him with it.

"Bastard!" she called him as she watched him foam at the mouth and die. "Knew there was something about you I didn't care for."

George had opened his eyes.

"Quiet," Sugar told him. "We gotta get you outta here."

She went to the door, cracked it open, and peeked outside. The other cop had not yet returned. She was not sure if he too was a fake cop and couldn't take any chances if he was. She had gotten lucky with this idiot, but the next man was way too large for her to take down herself. She closed the door to the room and went across the hall to the waiting room. She shook Lethia and her daughter to wake them up.

"Quiet," she said softly. "Come with me."

They all went into the room. George was sitting up now. He had unhooked himself.

"What's going on? Lethia said as she looked at the dead cop on the floor.

"He's a fake cop, probably one of Creed's men. We have to get out of here now. Help me move his body," she said, grabbing his arms. They dragged his body and put him in the closet. "OK, now look around for some drugs, any kind of painkillers. Morphine, hopefully. George is going to need it. And grab those bags of IVs they hooked up to him. Hurry, I'll be right back."

She opened the door and peeked down the hallway. The other cop was on his way back. There still was no one at the nurses' station. She slipped over, saw a nurse's coat on the rack, quickly put it on, and sat down. When the cop approached, she said "Come here, cutie. Got a message for you from your fellow officer."

He went over to her station and sat the coffee and donuts down. "What is it? Where did he go?"

Sugar was real sharp, and her beauty commanded attention. She knew this. She quickly made up a lie, hoping this wasn't one of Creed's men. "He got a call from your Captain Sanchez, I think. He said he needs you to meet him up on the fifth floor. Something going on up there with one of the patients, and a fight has broken out. The man's got a gun. Go now, I'll keep an eye on this guy. He's not going anywhere."

"Got it," he told her. "Thanks. Can I leave these here?"

"Sure thing," she told him. The cop was a real cop, not one of Creed's men. She felt relieved as he entered the elevator. Sugar grabbed a nearby wheelchair and wheeled it into the room. The two ladies helped George into it.

"Cover him up." Sugar said. Lethia had helped George get dressed while Sugar was dealing with the cop.

"Now what?" Lethia asked. "How do we get away from here?"

Sugar looked over at the closet where they had put the dead man. She walked over to the closet, told her daughter to turn away, and opened the door. The dead man's eyes were staring right at her, and then his hand moved. She jumped. It was nothing. It had just fallen. He was still dead. She began to search his pockets, feeling around his belt. "Got 'em," she said as she stood up with some keys. "Now we just have to find out which car they belong to. We have to hurry. That real cop's going to be back down here any second now once he realizes he's been duped."

"Oh yeah, forgot something." She looked at the floor, saw Creed's man's phone, and picked it up. "OK, let's go."

The four of them made their way downstairs undetected and out of the hospital.

*   *   *

Captain Sanchez had stayed behind after the trade to help with the dead and injured partiers from the rain. There were not as many casualties as first thought. The rain had come down fast and hard. A lot of the injuries were due to the sheer panic from the crowd. Once the rain stopped, the party continued, even though Sanchez and his men had tried to shut it down and get people to return to their homes. But the death count on the island was growing, and no one was paying attention. A lot of the dead were tourists, and because of the gag order, their families had not yet been notified. It was also going to take some time to identify some who had been badly mutilated, if it was even going to be possible, since all the bodies were being put in quarantine.

He needed some more answers. He was just about to call Tim when his phone rang. It was Tim. "Tim, what's going on? I was just about to call you."

"Got some good news and some bad. We've been found out and are getting ready to leave, that's the bad. The good news is that your partner's still alive. He's with us, but he's going to need a hospital fast. He's losing and has lost a lot of blood, and we can't move him. Creed's men are moving in. Not sure how they found us, but we have to go now."

"What do you mean that Caleb's there? I told him to go to the hospital hours ago."

"Sanchez," Tim butted in. "Did you hear what I just said? We've gotta go, and we can't move him."

"OK, Tim, I'll get some men there ASAP. I'm coming too. I'm looking at a bug I put on Creed. He's about fifteen minutes out, and it looks like he's heading your way, and with a small army, I'm sure. Do what you can for him, and you and the rest of your group get out of there. And tell me you people have found a solution to this parasite problem. I'll get some men together and head them off. Thanks, Tim, I'll meet up with you soon," Sanchez said as he ended his call. There was a tap on his shoulder.

"Was that Tim? What parasite problem? Is that what this is? Was that Tim Coles?" the sweet little voice from *News Now*'s Natasha Stevie asked.

"Put that down," Sanchez demanded as he grabbed for her phone, with which she was filming and recording him. He didn't succeed in getting the phone. "Not now, Natasha. I'm busy. You have to go get out of my way."

"Forget it, I heard enough, and I want some answers. Hell, we all do. Tim is my friend and coworker. And what about Marie? Are they OK? Are they alive? Come on, Sanchez, give me something, let me come with you," she was saying while running behind him.

"No way," he said. "And if you leak anything I just said or that you have on that phone, I'll bury you. Besides, I'm sure you've heard about the gag order pending an investigation."

"Let me come with you," she said, "or I'll send it to a friend in the States. They're not under gag orders, and I really don't care. My brother died on that beach the other day, and I need to know why."

Sanchez was about to pull off, and then he had a thought. "Do you have your news truck with you?"

"Yes, it's right over there."

Sanchez got out of his police car. "Come on, hurry. You drive."

CHAPTER 66

Alicia and George were outside now, slowly moving against the wall toward a figure that had his back turned. He was smoking a cigarette and looking at some porn on his phone. Alicia put her hand on George's chest to stop him from moving any farther while she quietly kept going. She took two more steps and pounced upon the man's back, putting one arm around his neck and the other on top of his forehead. George looked on in amazement, saying to himself, *What the fuck?* The man dropped his phone and cigarette. This was a large man, about six feet and three inches. Alicia was just about to snap his neck when she felt herself being flung over his head. She landed on her feet—part of her training. She turned around. George was about to come toward them, but Alicia Blake motioned for him to stay put.

"I got him," she said as she kicked the man in his knee, breaking his leg and then, with the padding of her palm, delivering a hard-driven uppercut to his jaw, thus breaking it. She then moved behind him again, putting one arm around his neck and the other on top of his forehead, and snapped his neck.

"Nice," George said. "Nice."

"Drag him behind that garbage can," Alicia said to him as she picked up his phone and stepped on his still-lit cigarette. "Search him for weapons and car keys."

She moved forward against the wall toward the front of the building. She surveyed the surroundings. Not seeing any more goons, she returned to where George was waiting. "I think we're clear, but I'm sure more are on their way. He just recently dialed someone, and I don't think it was hot girls."

George chuckled. "His SUV's right over there." He motioned as he made the lights flicker with the remote. "Hey, I gotta ask you something. Why do you think something's going on with my sister-in-law?

"She was texting someone all while your brother was explaining the parasites, and for someone who has just been kidnapped and released, that's not normal. Who's she texting? Isn't everyone with you guys on the island just about here?" she pointed out. "Don't trust her. I know a setup when I see one."

"Well, she's scared and a bit insecure. She thinks something is going on between my brother and your sister, so while you might be right, don't just snap her neck."

"Oh sorry, brother-in-law, but I'll fuck that bitch up when it comes to me protecting my sister. We got enough to deal with without being ratted on by one of our own. I mean, look, man, my sister and I appreciate you and your family helping out and all, but this shit goes deeper than you all can imagine. Five of my friends are dead. I have to take blame for that. My sister and I have both been used and betrayed. Not to mention what's happening. How we gonna stop this?"

"Don't know yet, but my brother's pretty sharp. I know him. He'll come up with something," George said as the two reentered the school.

"OK, gang, let's move it out," Alicia said. Everyone was waiting by the door when they came in—except Caleb, they had given him a gun and told him help was on the way. He was to shoot anyone he didn't know. The group inside had packed up some items from the lab that Louis and Sandra thought they might need.

"I suggest you and your family take the SUV. We can load these things in with you guys. The rest of you can go in Marie's car. I want to have a look around myself to see if there's anything else that might be useful, and I can help keep an eye out for our friend over there. I can't just leave him. He rescued me from that boat, and I owe him that much."

"Alicia," Sandra said. "Are you sure?"

"I'll be fine, go ahead. Creed surely has more men on their way."

Trish broke in. "Who put you in charge? This is all your fault. I'm not going anywhere. Tim just said help was on the way. I've made my own arrangements to leave all this behind." She turned to Louis. "I'm getting off this island tonight, and my children are coming with me."

"No, Ma, I'm staying with Dad. I heard you talking to that man who took us. I don't trust them," Lou Jr. said.

"Shut up," Lazarr said. "You're so stupid. I'm going with Mom. We're getting off the island tonight, dummy."

"Both of you stop it," Louis said. "Trish, don't do this. What did you do?"

Trish just turned and walked away. "Come on, kids, we're staying."

"Bro, we don't have time for this. We gotta go now," Little George said. He walked over to Trish, pulled a gun out of his back pocket, and gave it to her. "Good luck, sis."

Louis stood and watched as his wife and daughter walked away. Lou Jr. stayed with his father. Little George walked over to Alicia and whispered into her ear, "Promise me you won't hurt her."

"She's going to get herself killed, and the rest of you," she said back to him, "if you don't leave now. But it won't be by me."

Alicia hugged her sister. "Catch up with you in a minute. Now go."

Tim, Marie, and Tania were already in the car. George, Louis, Lou Jr., and Sandra headed for the SUV. They would follow Tim to where, who knew?

They were just pulling off when Creed and his men pulled up in a van and blocked them off. Creed, Damon, and three other men hopped out, guns drawn and pointed at the two vehicles. "Everyone out now," Creed demanded.

Alicia had heard the noise and was about to come back out of the school, ready to start shooting, when at that moment, a *News Now* van pulled up with two police cars in tow. Captain Sanchez got out, as did his officers, guns drawn and pointed at Creed and his men.

"Lower your weapons," Sanchez said.

Creed pointed his gun at Sanchez and said, "Stand down, captain. I have full jurisdiction for the arrest of these fugitives from the States."

"Not today, you don't. Move your van and let these people go." Sanchez stood firm.

Creed wasn't moving. He said again, "Captain, I have full jurisdiction. Check with your governor. But you and your men need to stand down now. Get out of my way before you get hurt."

"Is that so?" Sanchez said as he pointed Creed's attention to Natasha Stevie filming everything from the *News Now* van. "Are you ready to go live, Mr. Creed? Gunning down a police captain and his men?"

Creed glared at Natasha and then back at Sanchez. He motioned for his men to lower their weapons. "Damon, move the van. Let them go," he barked.

Trish was trying to get out of the school. Alicia Blake told her this man cannot be trusted. "This will all be over soon, don't go out there."

"Out of my way, you bitch," Trish said as she spit in Alicia's face. Alicia instantly grabbed Trish by the throat and was about to crush her windpipe when Lazarr grabbed the gun from her mother's purse and pointed it at Alicia.

"Let my mother go," she said, hands shaking.

Alicia stared at the young woman, not letting go of her mother. "Sweetie, you're gonna want to point that gun somewhere else, or I will snap her neck. Now," Alicia demanded.

Lazarr lowered the gun, and Alicia let Trish go and walked down the dark hallway. "Don't trust him. He's going to kill you if you do."

Alicia was gone. Trish and Lazarr went outside.

Tim and Louis had pulled off soon as Damon had moved out of the way. Louis did not see his wife come out. Creed walked over to Sanchez and lit a cigar. "You're way out of your league, island boy, and you're going to pay dearly for it."

He blew smoke into Sanchez's face and turned toward Natasha, pointing his finger at her like it was a gun. "Be seeing you around too, Ms. Weather Lady."

He threw his cigar on the ground, smashed it with his foot, and turned around. "Let's go, boys. Nothing left here. We got ourselves a meeting with the governor."

"Get in there. Now!" Sanchez ordered his men. They went into the school and found Caleb alive and awake. There was nothing and no one else. The ambulance Sanchez had called while they were en route had arrived and soon took Caleb. It was around five o'clock, time for the morning forecast.

CHAPTER 67

The owners of the tour companies and families of the dead and missing had gathered outside of the capital to demand some answers from Gov. Dirk Staten. He wouldn't come out. He'd sent his spokesperson to assure the crowd that they were making progress and that a statement would be coming soon. He also sent out all available officers to disperse the crowd.

"Go join the parade and festivities," the spokesperson reminded everyone. You could hear the grumbling as the crowd reluctantly left.

Creed was in the office with the governor. He'd given him a suitcase with US$2 million.

"Call off your captain now, or next time he interferes, I will kill him. Here is a statement for you to read to your people," Creed said as he passed him the piece of paper. "Read it as is, and I want a reward put on the Americans. This should flush them out. My men and I will conduct our own search. One more thing, there was a woman from the news filming us last night. Get that tape from her and make sure she doesn't have a voice on the news."

Creed said all this to the governor while he walked up to him, stared him down, and blew cigar smoke in his face. The governor immediately called the news station to ban Natasha Stevie from doing any type of broadcast. He also sent some men to detain her and get the footage.

*　　*　　*

The forecast called for clear skies and no chance of rain today. Tim and the rest of the group had taken refuge in a beautiful ranch-style home in Arashi, the smallest city in Aruba with a beautiful beach. Sugar, Brie, Lethia, and Big George were all there—everyone except Trish and Lazarr. Creed had them in a room back at the Marriott that Sofie had arranged. He questioned Trish to find out what they knew and what their plans were. Trish told him everything she knew, but they had not discussed a plan to stop the parasites. "That's all I know," she said.

"What about the shuttle parts? Who has them?" Creed demanded. "Do they have them with them?"

"I don't know," Trish said.

Her daughter broke in. "Yes, I saw them, they have them."

"Good," Creed said. "And do you know where they were going?"

"No," Trish and Lazarr answered.

"Now we've told you everything we know. Where is my money and our tickets to get off this island?" Trish said with no remorse toward her husband or the rest of the group. Creed nodded, and one of his goons brought a duffel bag filled with money.

"Here you are," Creed said as he opened the bag to show her the money. "One hundred thousand as agreed. My man will escort you and your daughter to the airport."

"What about my husband? You said—"

Creed cut her off. "He and the rest of them will be taken care of, and your son will be returned to you in the States. Don't worry, you've done the right thing. In fact, I'm sending one of my men to the States with you in case you have any trouble. You are aware you can't just board a plane with that large sum of money without raising eyebrows. He'll make sure you make it to Miami without being questioned, and then you're free to go anywhere you like. Here's my personal phone number. Take it and call only me, so I can return your son to you. Do we understand each other? I'm counting on your cooperation. You do know your son's life depends on it."

Trish nodded.

Creed handed the bag of money to his man. "Make sure they get to Miami without any problems. Give her the bag only once she leaves the airport, and then come back here."

"Goodbye, Ms. Alexander." He chucked with a smile. "Do enjoy your life. Oh, one more thing, wait at least a year before trying to cash in on your insurance policy for your husband. These things take time."

Creed and Damon watched as Trish, Lazarr, and their man left.

"Did you plant the device in the bag?" Creed asked Damon.

"Yes, sir. It will go off as soon as she flips through that bundle of $100 bills toward the bottom. That's one unhappily married bitch."

"Dead bitch," Creed said. "Dead bitch."

CHAPTER 68

"Can we go out and have some fun?" Lou Jr. asked his father.

"No, son. I don't think that's such a good idea," Louis said.

Lethia broke in. "I think it's a great idea. Don't you have something you should be working on, son? No need for the rest of us to stay cooped up in here. It's a lovely day, and I for one am tired of running from these animals. They're not going to stop, so you and your friends need to find a way to put an end to all this. Big George is resting. Come on, Sugar, let's go shopping."

"She's right," Tim said. "I don't think we all need to be here. We'll be harder to find if we're not all together. I'm sending Marie and my daughter somewhere safer. We're good for now, but it's a small island. Couple of days here at the most. I'm going to drop them off, grab a few things, check out what's going on weather-wise, and I'll be back in about eight hours."

Little George said, "I'll drop Sugar, Brie, and Mom off at Seaport Mall and keep Lou Jr. busy. I saw some BOB underwater scooters."

"Some what?" Louis asked.

"They're called BOB—Breathing Observation Bubble. You just wear a helmet, your head doesn't get wet, and you can breathe freely while checking out the seafloor or whatever's down there."

Louis knew it was a good idea to get everyone's mind off the tragic events that had taken place. He needed a break too. This was all so surreal to him. "OK," he said, "but everyone be careful. Try and blend in. Don't bring attention to yourselves."

"Please, everyone, pay with cash. I'm sure Lester is tracking your credit cards," Alicia said. "And I still need to tell you all something."

"It's going to have to wait, dear," Lethia responded. "We're out of here."

Sandra said, "I'm going to stick around, see if I can help Louis come up with something. But first I need a shower. Any fresh clothes around here, Tim?"

"Sure. Any of the five bedrooms have en suite showers, fresh clothes in the closet. That goes for all of you. Make yourselves at home. The bar is full. I'll be back in eight."

"That sounds great. Let's all get cleaned up," Sugar said. "We'll be ready in fifteen minutes." She was doing very well—after all, she had just killed someone. But she knew she had no choice. "Come shower with me." She grabbed her husband. "Fifteen minutes. We'll be back."

Louis was curious as to what Alicia wanted to tell them. He'd seen her bring in a duffel bag and sit it in the corner while the rest of the group put the items they had grabbed from the school in a little room Tim had pointed out. He went to the fridge. There was cold beer inside, so he grabbed two and went outside. It was a beautiful day. He went to the back of the house, where three stairs down was the beach, and walked to the right, to a private swimming pool. The outside also boasted a beautiful thirty by thirty Arman tree with an attached hammock and swing. There was also an implanted cement table, a picnic table, an assortment of six colorful chairs (ranging from blue, yellow, red, and pink), and three lounge chairs. The villa was set on its own private beach, with nothing short of a spectacular snapshot view of the ocean. The waves were calming for him. The sound helped clear his head and allowed him to focus. He walked to the tip of the water. Small crabs scattered across the finely raked sand, hiding in their holes.

Louis glared at the sea and the sky. No clouds in sight. His mind was racing. He'd come up with something that might just work.

Alicia appeared on the beach next to him. "I just checked on your dad. He's fine and resting. The rest of your family just took off. I'm really sorry about your wife and daughter, but listen, I have to get this off my conscience. I feel partly responsible for getting you guys involved in all this."

"All this death," he said, "for what? Why couldn't NASA just admit they screwed up? No one knew what was up there. Hell, most people believe something's out there anyway, why not just contain it?"

"You have to ask Sandra that one. Look, I see you're deep in thought. I'll get back to you guys later," she said as she turned and walked away.

Louis was feeling some type of way. He felt betrayed but also felt relief. He knew this trip was a long shot to try to put his marriage back together, but it was just now that it was really over, and he knew it. They had talked about divorce before, but neither had moved on it. Now he knew it was time. Louis headed back to the house, needing a shower himself. He felt dirty, sticky. He walked into one of the bedrooms and began taking off his clothes—shoes first, and then he pulled his shirt over his head while walking into the bathroom.

He looked up. Sandra was standing there, drying her hair, completely naked. Her body glowed. Her breasts were firm. He didn't move. She looked over and saw him.

"Sorry, I didn't know anyone was in here."

She didn't cover herself up. She looked him dead in his eyes. "It's OK," she said. "Can you pass me that towel behind you?"

Louis grabbed the towel. He felt aroused. He was comfortable with this woman, as if he could tell her anything. He'd never had this feeling before. He handed her the towel and was about to leave.

"You don't have to go. I'm all done in here, The shower's yours. I'll just be a few minutes more," she said as she wrapped herself in the towel. She knew he liked what he saw, and she liked him too. "What are your thoughts?"

"My thoughts?" he stuttered.

"Yes, about how to get rid of the parasites," she said as she moved away from the shower. "All yours. Shy type? Go ahead, I don't bite, really."

She took a step toward him. "Soap's in the dish."

Louis let his shirt fall to the floor. He moved toward the shower and let his pants fall while stepping in.

"Nice ass," Sandra said.

Louis had turned on the water. "What did you say?" he shouted as the water hit his head.

"Never mind."

He felt relaxed now as he lathered himself up with soap. His manhood was still aroused. He couldn't get the image of her naked glowing body standing right before him out of his head. Yes, he wanted her.

She opened the shower door. He stood there, penis standing at attention. She glanced at his manhood. "You need this," she said as she handed him some shampoo.

"Yeah, thanks."

She closed the door and left the bathroom. He finished showering. When he stepped out the bathroom, she was sitting on the bed applying sunblock on her body.

"Can you get my back?"

"Sure." He stepped over to her with the towel wrapped around his waist. She turned her back to him. He slowly started to rub her back. Her skin was soft to the touch, her shoulders firm. She moved her hair out of the way so he could get to the back of her neck. His hands were firm, she thought. She liked the way they felt.

"Now you," she said. "Turn around."

She grabbed his hand and slowly removed the sunblock lotion from it. "Lie down on your stomach," she instructed him.

He did. Without warning, she was sitting on the back of his thighs. She squirted lotion on his back. He shivered.

"Cold, right?" She giggled.

Who is this woman? he thought to himself. Her hands were soft to the touch. What was happening? He wasn't sure, but it felt good to have someone touch him, someone pay him some attention. He liked it.

She got off him. "There you are. The rest you can do yourself." She had found a tank top and slipped it on along with some shorts. "What's to drink?" she said as she headed for the bedroom door. "I believe the men's closet is over there. Can you believe this place? It's fully stocked."

"So is the bar," Louis replied. "Would you mind fixing me a margarita on the rocks?"

"For sure," she said.

CHAPTER 69

The carnival was in full swing. Thousands of partygoers packed the streets, bands were playing, and the floats and costumes were magnificent. Beaches were full. The island was active. The day was young. The skies were clear.

Natasha Stevie was furious—she couldn't believe she was being suspended. She'd been told she was interfering in an investigation of National Security and was forced to give up her footage, but being the savvy newswoman she was, she had already made a backup.

Creed wasn't new to his profession either, and he figured she would, and that's why he was having her followed. Natasha was on her way to the hospital to see Sanchez. He was there checking on Caleb, who was now stable and doing much better. In fact, they were going to release him later that day. Sanchez also found out about the men Creed had posing as officers. The body of the man Sugar had been forced to kill had been discovered. Sanchez himself was taken off the case and suspended. He knew the governor had probably been paid off. What an asshole. He was going to have to pay and answer for all these deaths and missing people.

The northern side of the island was temporally quarantined. Police had discovered some terribly mutilated missing tourist remains and several empty buses at the Gold Mill Ruins. But no one was talking about it. One of his loyal officers had tipped him off even though he'd been suspended. Sanchez knew there had to be more missing tourists.

Creed and Damon, having no luck on the beach-friendly side of the island, went to a popular tourist attraction, ABC Safari. The company gave off-road tours of the north side of the island, making stops at the California Lighthouse, the Natural Pool, the Alto Vista Chapel, and more. He now had at least fifty men on the island searching for the twins and the Alexander family, but mostly Tim Coles and Sandra Blake. He confiscated ten company Jeeps along with drivers to guide his men throughout the northern side, making sure to dispose of any and all evidence of death along the way. Everything was being covered up and written off as if nothing had ever happen.

The US government was working with Aruba to pay hush money to the families of the dead and injured. The cruise line had come up with some bullshit story about how the captain and his crew had hijacked the missing ship and were currently in custody in Guantanamo Bay, accused of planning to rob and murder the passengers. None of this was true, but he still could not prove it wasn't. It sounded absolutely absurd, but he had no proof of the explanation he was being given by the Alexander group either, even though he'd seen what had happened when the rainfall came. It was time to get the proof he needed.

Caleb said he was ready to leave now. Sanchez tried to get him to wait, but he refused. He got plenty of painkillers from the hospital, a good prescription, and the two men walked out, neither with any legal authority to do anything, since Caleb was now officially on medical leave after being shot in the line of duty. A full investigation was going on, but there were no bodies to confirm his story, said the governor. The two men were no closer to finding out the truth than they were when they got the distress call from the *Two of Us*. All they knew for sure was that Lester Creed had to be stopped. Sanchez told Caleb about the standoff with Creed and his men and how he needed to find the group. He also told him about Natasha filming the whole thing, which was probably the only reason he and the rest of them were alive.

They were waiting for Natasha to get there when they heard a call go out over the police band about a car on fire a couple of miles from them.

"No, please don't let it be," Sanchez said. He dialed Natasha's phone and didn't get an answer. "Please, no."

Just at that moment, Natasha pulled up. "Sorry, I'm late. There was a car fire just down the road."

"Come with us, Natasha." Sanchez spotted the men following her as the three of them pulled off in his cruiser. "We have company."

*　　*　　*

"Yes, what is it?" Damon said into the phone.

"She just got into a car with two men at the hospital. They're pulling off now. What do you want us to do, sir?" The man was on speaker. Creed heard him as Damon looked over to him for instructions.

"Follow them, you idiot. Don't lose them, and don't let them spot you," Creed barked. He pushed the girl up from between his legs, stood up, pulled her to his cock, and let his load explode in her mouth. He put his cigar out, threw $200 on the chair, put on his pants, and sent the hooker on her way. "Pull the van around, Damon. We have work to do."

CHAPTER 70

It was starting to get late in the day. The night scene would be on full blast. The island never stopped partying. It would be easier to move around after sunset, normally around six fifty-three. The beach would still be full of people gazing at the beautiful allure of the sunset, the sunset cruises, and the bars getting ready for evening partygoers and diners. Shoppers would also come out to make their best deals with the street vendors. For Louis and the crew, there were things to do besides that, though.

He thought he had a way to end this travesty, get the truth out, and perhaps get his family back. No, he shook his head. Better forget that last part. His marriage was done, and he knew it. Better start anew, perhaps with Sandra. He shook his head again. Was it too soon to even be thinking like this? He couldn't help it, and he couldn't get this afternoon out of his mind. There was no doubt she had some type of feeling for him. He decided to go check on Big George, see if he needed anything. He could see Sandra and Alicia walking back from the lighthouse, another beautiful tourist attraction from where you could see the whole island and the sky.

"That's it," he said out loud to himself. "We can track the cloud from there." He would have to check with Tim, he was the weather expert, but it should work. Louis walked into the room, and a cold sensation overcame him. It was dead quiet and stale smelling. He walked over to George and shook him.

"You OK, G?" he said, as he would sometimes call him. There was nothing. His body felt stiff. His eyes were closed. He shook him again, this time harder. "Yo, G, wake up."

Nothing. Louis stood over him, and then he put both hands on him and began to shake him even harder. His commands for him to wake up got louder. Still, there was no response. Sandra and Alicia came into the room. They had heard him shouting. Sandra walked over to him and checked his breathing by putting her head close to his mouth and nose.

"Nothing," she said. His chest was not rising nor falling. She grabbed his wrist and held it for fifteen seconds. Nothing. She turned to Louis and shook her head. "I'm sorry, he's gone."

She gently put Big George's arm on his chest. Alicia had spotted some spare sheets on the other side of the room, so she grabbed them and brought them over to cover the deceased man. Sandra grabbed Louis by the hand and led him out of the room over to the bar. He hadn't said anything. He just had a blank kind of stare. Sandra passed him a margarita on the rocks. She poured herself one too, and one for her sister. She lifted her glass. "Here's to Big George. He saved us back at that hotel. I'm sorry for your loss, Louis. I'm sorry for all this."

Louis downed his glass, walked into the other room, and grabbed something out of the bags from the college. He went back into the room with George's body. He couldn't have been dead long, he thought to himself. He locked himself in the room and then uncovered George's left arm. With a dissecting scalpel, he meticulously cut deep into the elbow. Warm, smelly blood squirted onto his face and shirt. It was done. He removed the elbow from the dead man and wrapped it in a pillow case. He was just about to leave the room when he heard the sound of laughter approaching. It was the rest of the clan outside.

He went out a door leading outside from the bedroom and reentered the house from the front. Dammit, he forgot to unlock the door. He went to the deep freezer he spotted in the kitchen and placed the dripping, bloody arm inside. He eased himself back outside and into the room.

"Sorry, G," he said as he looked over at the dead man. He unlocked the door and came out the room. They were back.

Lou Jr. ran over to his dad. "Dad, you should've been there. Uncle George took me on the BOBs and the James Bond thing."

"The what?" his father asked.

"The James Bond thing."

"Not sure what you're talking about, son, but it appears you all had a good time."

"It's called a sea BOB, bro. It's an underwater scooter just like the ones in the old James Bond movies. Cool as hell."

"Hey, George, got something I need to tell you all—"

Before he could finish, they heard a scream coming from the back room. It was their mother. She'd gone to check on Big George.

"He's gone, bro. Passed away in his sleep. There was nothing we could do."

Little George and Sugar went to the back room where their mother was weeping. He sat her down on the bed. "It's gonna be all right, Mom."

She looked at him. "Are you sure, son? Can you be absolutely sure? You boys stay here and do what you have to do to end this and help save these people on this island, but it's time for me to take my leave. Sugar, you and my grandson and granddaughter should come with me."

"OK, Ma, you're right. You take Lou Jr."

"No, Dad, I'm staying with you. I can help. You always taught me not to run from your troubles but to face them. I'm not going to run. I'm staying."

Lethia giggled as she wiped a tear from her face. "Yep, that's your son, all right."

"I believe I can help with that," Alicia said. "But first, I've been trying to say something to all of you for the last couple of days. I'm not sure if this is the right time, but I have to say it."

"Say what?" a voice came from the back entrance. It was Tim. "What's going on?"

CHAPTER 71

In Miami, Trish and Lazarr had been escorted through customs by Creed's goon. He handed her the bag full of money and watched as they made their exit from the airport and got into a cab. It was early, about 10:00 a.m.

"What should we do first?" Lazarr asked her mother.

"Well, first we're going to check into a fine hotel, get cleaned up, rent a Benz, and go shopping. Take me to the Faena Hotel Miami Beach," she gloated to the driver, acting as if she were high society. She was dying to open the bag, but she knew she should wait until they were settled in. It didn't take long for them to get there. She checked in and poured herself a drink while Lazarr showered. They had bought some clothes from the fancy gift shop before actually going up to the room. She used her credit card. No need to hide anymore.

She felt no remorse for her husband. Her thoughts were on the money, the insurance policy, and the good life that she thought she deserved. Oh, she did want her son back. The rest of his family could go to hell or all die. She never really cared for them. She always felt like an outcast. That had changed now. She had money—lots of it and with more to come.

Lazarr was out of the shower now. She was old enough, so she poured herself a drink and went out to the balcony where her mother was.

"Try this, darling," her mother said. "I had the butler bring some lobster and a fresh bottle of wine. I'm going to shower, and then we'll open the bag together and go shopping."

"All right, Mother. But hurry, I want to post a picture on Facebook."

CHAPTER 72

The skies had been clear all day. Evening had set in. Everyone was at the new villa Tim had supplied though one of his friends. Although he had told them all they would only be safe here for a few days, everyone felt relaxed as they could possibly be. It was time to get out, Louis thought. He needed to get some more supplies to test his theory. That's when his brother came out the room where his father lay dead.

"What happened to him?"

At almost the same moment, there was a scream from the kitchen. It was Little George's daughter, Brie. She was crying.

"What's wrong?" her mother asked.

"There's an arm in the freezer."

"What?" her mother said.

"Wait, I can explain," Louis was saying to everyone as his younger brother, who stood about six feet and weighed in at around 220 pounds, grabbed him and pushed him to the floor, having spotted the blood on his shirt.

"That's exactly what I was about to ask. I just noticed his arm has been cut off."

Louis got up and pushed his brother back. "Look, dammit, all of you, just wait. Give me a minute to explain," he was saying when his brother punched him in the mouth.

Louis was no stranger to fights. He and his brother had fights in their childhood, he was much smaller at five feet seven and a half inches. Louis quickly grabbed his throat while pulling the scalpel out and holding it to him. He moved his brother to a nearby couch and pushed him down on it. Their mother was screaming for them to stop.

"I said let me explain."

Alicia was about to fire off her gun when Sandra grabbed her. Tim had gone into the room and was saying to himself, "Motherfucker, there's blood all over the floor." He stood in the bedroom doorway waiting to hear Louis explain why he had cut off the dead man's arm, the man who had sacrificed his life for them. Sugar, Brie, Lou Jr., and Lethia all sat down on the couch.

Tears were falling from Lethia's eyes. The family was exploding. This was all too much. It just reasserted what she'd said earlier: it was time to get off this island.

"Look, everyone, I'm sorry you had to find out this way. First, Big George was already gone. He died from his injuries. You all know I could never do anything like that."

"Um, you look pretty handy with that scalpel to me," Alicia mumbled to her sister, who in return glared at her.

"But I had no choice. I need his arm to conduct some tests. I put together a working theory on how to fight off and hopefully kill the parasites, but it's just that until I can test it, a theory. And I'm sorry, bro, Mom. He meant a lot to me too, but let his sacrifice continue to help us put an end to this thing and stop the real monster running around the island, *Lester Creed*."

"He's right," Sandra said. "Creed's not going to stop."

Tim moved to the middle of the room. "For that matter, folks, neither is the rain. I did some tracking while I was away, and it doesn't get any better from here. The carnival is in full swing, and the nimbostratus clouds are moving in."

Alicia saw some movement outside. She was very edgy. Tim saw this. "Hold on, they're OK. It's only the villa gardeners. They rake the beach every morning and provide security at night for the guests who stay here. I asked them to go out earlier and collect some wood to make a bonfire for us tonight. I'm truly sorry about your loss. He was a brave man. Maybe you guys want to do some type of visual in his honor around the fire. And as hard as it may be for you to swallow this right now, we have to get rid of the body. I suggest we lay him to rest in the ocean. We can use the boat tied to the tree outside. I know the owner keeps it for emergencies."

"Fine," Little George said. "Only if it's OK with Mom."

Lethia just shook her head now, trying to hold back the tears. "It's OK. You boys take care of this. That monster better be made to pay for what he's done. We'll all say a few words in his honor around the bonfire." She looked at her sons with that mother's look. "Agreed?"

"Yes," Louis said.

"All right, we're good," Little George said as he grabbed his brother and hugged him. "We're good."

"*Wow*, I need a drink," Alicia said as she made her way to the bar, still looking at the two gardeners, Jordan and Delardo, as they were setting up the fire. Still, she had not been able to share her guilt about her part in this.

"I'm still going to have to get out and get some things I need. I was hoping you guys could help me out with that," Louis was saying to Tim as he watched Sandra over at the bar filling her drink. She looked back at him and began to fix him a margarita. "Especially you, Tim."

Sandra said, "I'm in. I think we adults could all use a night out."

"Yes," they all chimed in.

"You youngsters go ahead, I'll stay with the kids," Lethia said.

As much as Sugar didn't want to let her husband go, especially with Alicia joining them, she declined. "I'm just going to stay here with Lethia and the kids."

She pulled her husband to the side. "Find us a way off this island tonight. We'll wait for you. I love you." She kissed him. "Help your brother and these people end this horror and death."

The bonfire was ready. Everyone moved outside to the fire and made a circle. Each of the family took turns speaking of Big George. Afterward, everyone loaded the body into the inflatable rubber boat and headed out to the dark sea.

CHAPTER 73

The carnival was going into its final week. Things were really picking up now. Lester Creed and his men were no closer to finding the sisters or anyone in the family than when he and Damon first started, and he knew it was because of Tim Coles. He had them in his grasp until that fucking Captain Sanchez and the news bitch showed up.

He and Damon were at Matt's beachside restaurant, drinking. He was waiting for the local news to come on. Governor Staten was about to come on and issue a US$10,000 reward for any information leading to the arrest of Alicia Blake, Sandra Blake, and now, listed as alive and as cohorts of the sisters, the island's very own Tim Coles, plus the members of the Alexander clan. Photos of all the above were being passed around the island. They were being listed as armed and dangerous and as terrorists associated with what was being officially called C.M.W.W.—Chemical Manipulation Weather Warfare. This was used to explain the chemicals or acid-like rain. Pictures were being circulated all over the island, and anyone coming in contact or seeing any of these individuals were being asked to call this hotline number flashing on their TV screens or the police right away.

Governor Staten also went on to say, Sofie standing by his side during the broadcast, that locals and tourists should go about their daily activities and excursions. They should enjoy the carnival because the situation was under control. He also said the police and locals should fully cooperate with Lester Creed and his men, who were here to help and apprehend these dangerous terrorists.

"That's it, Damon. That should flush them out." Creed smiled as he lit a cigar and ordered another drink. "What's the status on the wife and daughter? Any booming news?" he shrieked, laughing out loud.

* * *

Louis had still periodically been attempting to contact his wife and daughter. He feared the worst but hoped for the best, even if it was over between them. He still got nothing. He wondered if she still even had the phone. The group had decided to go on a night excursion. The "drunk bus," he called it.

Locals called it Kukoo Kunuku. The bus did a pub crawl, barhopping at local bars off the tourist scene. He could explain his plan to everyone at one of the four bar stops, where they also gave you a complimentary shot. It also stopped at the lighthouse for a champagne toast to get the party started. While at the lighthouse, he discovered there was a radar tower right next to it that he thought they could use to warn other cruise ships and prevent them from coming in contact with the deadly cloud.

While walking down Ashanti Beach earlier, Alicia and Sandra said they spotted hundreds of seagulls diving really close to the rocks. They also said they chatted with the neighbors' (Otis and Ruth Nelson) sons, a couple of stoners at the home next to the villa they were now hiding out at. They claimed they had seen the missing cruise ship go down after a scary-looking cloud appeared above it. They said they reported it, but no one believed them because they were always high. Therefore, the coast guard or anyone else never searched the area they spoke of. Arrest had reportedly been made anyway of the captain and his crew. The sons also claimed to have seen a small boat close to shore go down as they were crab fishing. They even claimed to have tried to warn them as the cloud moved in over them, but the fisherman just waved at them, and the brothers ran in the house as the fisherman came to their demise. So if their bones had washed up to the rocks, that could be what the seagulls were feeding on.

"*Wow*," Louis said. "Sounds crazy enough to be true. You can see the ships out at sea go by that location." At the third stop, they were able to get a table in the back, away from the crowd. Everyone was pretty toasted. Louis began by telling them what he thought would kill the parasites. "We just need some hot tea, coconut oil, garlic, and cloves, and then—then we'll need containment booms and skimmers, explosives, and lots and lots of tequila."

"He's drunk, right? Are you kidding me? What in the fuck are you going to do with that shit?" Tim slurred.

"Sounds like he's thinking about the bats in the cave. Garlic, bro?" George laughed while downing another drink.

Sandra grabbed Louis. "Come on, let's dance."

She was pulling him out of his seat when Alicia said, "*I have explosives!*"

Louis felt a chill come over his body and run down his spine. A sour taste filled his stomach, and saliva built up in his throat. "I feel like I need to vomit," he said while spitting on the floor.

"Come on, bro, I got you." George grabbed his brother and headed for the bathroom. The music was loud. Most of the bus patrons were loading up to head to the next stop.

*   *   *

Trish and Lazarr were both tipsy. The money was all over the king-sized bed with 100 percent mulberry silk sheets.

"Seventy-five thousand," Lazarr counted.

"OK, honey." Trish picked up another bundle of hundreds. She flipped through the bills.

Louis tried to vomit, but nothing came out.

There was a violent explosion at the Faena Hotel that sent flames bursting through the windows, sending glass down to the streets.

Damon's smart watch started to chime. "It's done, boss."

*   *   *

The drunk bus was leaving its last stop. Louis was feeling better. He had stopped drinking for the night. He felt uneasy. Something was wrong, and he could feel it. They were all back at the villa now. It was about twelve, and the bonfire was still burning but low. The ocean was dark. You could still hear the sounds of the waves coming in. It was soothing yet had a significant sound. Louis was just sitting in a chair watching the flames. The wood from the bonfire was crackling. Tim, Sandra, Alicia, and George came out and sat with him.

"You OK, bro?"

"Yes," he said, "but I can't help but feel something bad has happened."

"Finish telling us your plan for dealing with the clouds," Alicia said. "I told you all I have explosives."

"Yes, you did," Louis said. "But why? And just what is it that you keep saying you have to share with us?"

Alicia went on to tell the story of how she had known about Sandra's work at NASA and how she had read through her sister's files one night when they had been drinking. She also revealed that she too sometimes had been contacted by NASA to retrieve space junk. This time, she contacted them only after learning from some salvage guys that something was lost out here in the Caribbean Sea. "I needed the money, and knew I could make this my last dive. I have to, because of my blackouts."

Sandra was furious. "So you used me!" she shouted.

"Look, I didn't mean for any of this to happen. I was trying to get out. My doctor bills are enormous, and I didn't want to burden you, so I took this last job."

"What exactly is the job?" Little George butted in.

"The last missing part of the shuttle has been traced here. My job is to destroy it. I promise you all, I didn't know anything about a Lester Creed or a cover-up. I was searching for the last piece of shuttle when my friends died. I'm sorry for everyone's loss. Sandra, you were not supposed to be here. I'm sorry," Alicia again said, pushing back her tears while looking at her sister. "Now we need to finish this. I know how to get the rest of your family off the island. Tell me your theory to stop the parasites. Let me help end this."

"This shit just keeps getting better and better," Tim exclaimed.

"OK, here it is. It's a long shot, and we're going to need a lot of help." Louis went on to explain how when there's an oil spill, they used booms and skimmers to trap the oil. "In this scenario, we need to trap a certain body of water that we can fill with ecofriendly chemicals, and then we pull them under the cloud and hope it's hot enough for some of the chemicals to evaporate into the nimbo cloud. The rest, we set off an explosion, strong enough to reach the cloud by using various firework-type techniques. We have to try to kill the parasites while out there above the water, of course, so Tim, I'll need to know how many knots or miles per hour the wind is moving, so we can set up and be able to move with the clouds."

"Assuming this works, what about when it does hit landfall and if they're scattered?" Sandra asked.

"Well, before all this even occurs, brother, where do you propose we get all this shit from to even set off this type of operation? And how much of it do we need?"

"I need the best possible ten-day forecast I can get from you, Tim. Some of it I know we can get on the island, the rest—"

Alicia broke in. "The rest, leave it up to me. Get me a detailed list of everything you need and how much, I can get it. Get it to me tomorrow, and give me a day to get it. And have your family ready to leave in the morning."

"Where are you planning to take them and how are you going to get them off the island? The airport and cruise ships are being watched," George said.

"The less everyone knows about it, the safer we all are. You're coming along anyhow. Need those muscles."

Louis continued, "We're going to have to be prepared to detour the carnival routes depending on cloud movement, so we're going to need signs, cones, and, more than anything, people for parade marshals to work with us. I have a plan for land. Still working on it, but it will at the least minimize death to injuries. We may still have casualties if we can't get them to follow the detours."

"We have another problem," Sandra said. "Anyone see this?" She was looking at her phone. "This looks like some type of amber alert, but it's for all of us. We're all wanted terrorists."

CHAPTER 74

Sanchez, Caleb, and Natasha stopped at an ice cream stand near Seaport Mall in the downtown area. The three of them got out of the car, ordered ice cream, and took a seat.

Creed's men were pulled over about 100 feet away, watching them. It was crowded downtown. More cruise ships had come in, and the passengers were busy shopping.

Sanchez had made a call to a couple of the night girls he knew would be in the area. They too had something to sell to willing passengers who were looking for a little bit more excitement. The two women were talking to Creed's men when Sanchez hopped into the back of their car, gun in hand, and relieved the two of their weapons and phones. He told them to drive up to the ice cream shop.

Caleb and Natasha got back into their car and headed to a secluded spot not on Creed's watch list where they could interrogate the men.

CHAPTER 75

It was about eight in the morning. A few clouds were moving in toward the vendors setting up on the beach.

*   *   *

It had been a long night. Several things had transpired late night at the villa. Tim was up after everyone went their separate ways. When the bonfire died out, he called to check on Marie and his daughter. They were fine, hidden away from all this. He assured her he was OK and it would all be over soon. But he was watching the clouds move in from the east. It started out with about five clouds. They were separated at first, and then he could see they were being pulled together. He could also see the faint blue and green flashing lights, possibly nimbostratus clouds. He kept watching. This cloud formation was different. The wind was moving the clouds in a whirlwind in the sky. More scattered clouds were attaching themselves to the other cloud, and then they would disappear and reappear back over the island. It was a like some sort of sky pool trapped in a circular whirlwind because of the electromagnetic radiation. The radiation in the parasites would not allow the clouds to move beyond Aruba's geographical pull, and they looked to be heading for Palm Island.

*   *   *

Louis had given Alicia the big list. That morning, he and Sandra were walking on the beach, on their way back from the market where he had purchased things he needed to test his theory on Big George's now-thawed arm. On the beach, he could feel something different in the trade winds blowing the sand in the water. If briefly felt like the sand was cutting into him. The waves were kicking up pretty hard. Minute by minute, the beach was filling up—walkers were walking, joggers were jogging. He worried about the death and devastation if his theory didn't work.

No one had spotted them so far, they thought, as they were approaching the villa. They went into a back room he had set up, and he made the mixture from the list of things he'd gotten. The idea was simple. Basically, he was using a formula on how to kill parasites in humans. He took the arm and cut off a small portion of muscle tissue connected to the bone. He put it under the microscope, and then he released some of the live parasites they had kept in containment. They quickly were feasting though the muscle tissue while their radioactive nucleus just plainly disintegrated everything else except the bones. He carefully spread the mixture over the feasting parasites, careful not to come in contact with them. Then they waited and observed.

*   *   *

Alicia's plan to get Lethia, Sugar, and Brie off the island was hardly simple. She had contacted and called in debts owed to her by a salvaging company and a treasure hunter friend in Venezuela. Venezuela was only 772 kilometers (20 miles) from Aruba. She thought that since NASA and the US government were trying to put the blame on them, they should want to help. She knew they were watching the airlines and cruise ships.

The Dutch Caribbean Coast Guard (DCCG) only had three support centers, and they were mainly concentrated on Aruba, Curacao, and Saint Maarten, handling maritime distress, search, and rescue. Most excursions stayed within their boundaries. At night, they patrolled for Detection and Drug Control as well as Customs Control at sea. Creed was working with them. Her plan was to hijack the *Atlantis* submarine vessel after its last excursion for the evening and force the captain to take her along with Little George and the others to Venezuela. There, they would have her contact get the family to a safe house. Then she could get the remaining supplies in bulk that her friend would supply and have ready, get it loaded at the salvaging company, dock and head back to Aruba, and hopefully pay the captain to keep him quiet, or detain him until this was all over. Oh, and if they were caught, she would simply threaten to blow everything and everyone up. She knew no one in the group would agree to this, so that's why she decided not to tell them her elaborate plan.

*   *   *

Little George had moved his family, his mother, and Lou. Jr, who was still insisting on staying with his father, to another location that morning on Tim's request. It was to be everyone's last day at the Idle Hours Villa. They were really chancing it now that they were all wanted and had their pictures plastered all over the island, but it was still easy to move around. Most tourists who were coming in and leaving daily didn't pay much attention to what was happening. He had successfully moved Lethia, Sugar, Brie, and Lou Jr. to a resort off the beach where he knew the manager. The Caribbean Palms Villa was secure and private, about a mile from Eagle Beach and directly across the street from the police station. No one would be looking there.

Little George and Tim were on the porch, overlooking the sea. Alicia was lying in the hammock when she noticed that Jordan and Delardo, the gardeners, were still there. Jordan was on the phone, and Delardo seemed to be watching them from the gate leading to the main street, as if he were waiting for someone. This seemed strange to her because they normally had been raking the sand early in the morning, and it was now well after noon. She quickly went over to Tim and told him to get Louis and Sandra. She told George to start loading the boat tied to the tree. At first, Tim smirked and thought she was just being paranoid, and then he thought about the reward being offered.

Alicia quietly snuck up on Jordan and hit him on the back of the head with her gun, knocking him out. She grabbed his phone. A van pulled up at that moment, and Alicia started shooting at the van and Delardo.

"What the fuck's going on?" Louis was saying as he and Sandra loaded the last of the equipment into the boat.

Creed, Damon, and three other men hopped out of the van, returning gunfire at them. Little George started shooting back.

"Let's move it!" Alicia shouted. She had them pinned down for the moment.

"Don't let them get away! Get them!" Creed was shouting at his men as he pushed one of them out from the side of the van, only to see him struck down by a bullet to the head and throat. "Kill them, kill them all!"

Tim had the boat started and was waiting for Alicia and George.

"Go on!" Alicia shouted at George. "I'll cover you!"

George ran through the sand toward the boat. He caught a bullet to the side but managed to climb into the boat. Alicia pulled out a grenade and pulled the pin, all while making a dash for the boat. She threw the grenade at Creed's other two men who were shooting at her, all while shooting back at them herself. She got to the boat as the grenade went off, killing the two men and rocking the van where Creed and Damon were still ducking for cover.

Tim sped out to sea. The smoke and fire could be seen for a few miles from the beachgoers and the lighthouse. Neighbors from across the road came out.

Creed and Damon got in the van and left.

"I want them dead, all of them! Have some men come and search the villa for the scraps now!" Creed was hollering wildly. "Motherfucking bitch! Did she just throw a fucking grenade at me? *I want them found, and I want them dead!*"

"Where are we going now?" Louis asked Tim, who was driving the cutter boat. "My brother's been shot."

"To a place where I don't think they will be looking, and where perhaps we can get some answers. There's a dock there for the rich folk that live in the private gated community, it's called Cal Di Solo. Sofie Labridge lives there, and we can patch your brother up. The bullet just grazed him."

CHAPTER 76

Caleb and Natasha were following Creed's two men with Sanchez in their back seat. They had made their way to a little house nested in the desert not far from the Alto Vista Chapel and less than five miles from where he'd heard on his police radio about the gunfire and explosion at the villa. He knew Creed had to be involved. He just hoped that Tim and the rest of them were still alive and safe. He also he saw a group text from Damon to the rest of Creed's men to search the area around the lighthouse and radar tower, saying the cutter boat was spotted heading that way. He had to find out what these men knew, and quick. They needed to get to Tim before Creed did.

After pulling off one of the men's fingernails and badly beating the other, Sanchez decided they didn't know enough and thought it best to move on. They left the men bloodied and tied to each other in a locked little pantry. He would come back for them later. Damon had tried calling the two and couldn't get through. Sanchez took a picture of the two bloody men and sent it back to the number from which it came, with only the message "YOUR TIME IS NEAR, MR. CREED."

"Let's go," Sanchez said as the three of them got into their car and headed for the area he thought Creed would be looking into. He also thought about heading for the greedy bitch's house who also lived in that area, Sofie.

The gated community had a twenty-four–hour guard. With the group listed as terrorists, they would need some type of diversion to distract the marine guard to get in, Tim told the others.

"Give me five minutes with him," Alicia said, "while you tie down the boat." Alicia Blake knew her beauty called attention to her, and most men were intimidated by it. She swayed directly for the guard shack. No one else was around. This was no diversion. She pulled out her gun, stepped into the guard shack, and forced the man to his knees as he begged for his life. Alicia took some duct tape from her backpack, taped his mouth shut, and secured his hands and feet. She was just about to leave when she decided she had better render him unconsciousness. She decided to use the method known as the Chinese stranglehold to cut off the blood flow to the brain. She wasn't trying to kill the man and had used this method many times before. This should allow Tim enough time to get whatever information he'd hoped to get from her. If it were up to her, she would just beat it out of Sofie.

Time was also becoming a factor. She had to get to that submarine before the captain took off for the night. The streets were crowded and full because of the carnival being in full swing. She motioned for everyone to come on, as the coast was clear.

Sofie wasn't expecting anyone, and there had been no call from the guard when a knock on the door startled her. She took her suitcase with her half of the payoff of US$1 million and set it in the closet. Again, a knock came. Sofie grabbed her full wine glass and headed for the door. She was dressed in some shorts and a tank top that showed the lower portion of her breasts through the side, her full cleavage, and the full shape of her nipples. She looked out her peephole. Tim Coles? How did he get here? What did he want?

She backed away from the door and was going for her phone when Sandra, Louis, and George came in from the back. Louis went and opened the front door. Sandra said, "You would think to lock your back door. You never know what terrorists might be lurking, according to you and the governor. Isn't that right, Ms. Sofie Labridge?"

"Where's your bathroom? We need to fix him up," Sandra said, referring to George. "You almost got us killed with your lies, bitch."

Sofie's home was beautiful. It was on a magnificent golf course estate and had three bedrooms, two bathrooms, and 9,687.53 square feet of land. It had a two-floor plan with a formal living room and formal dining room that opened to a gourmet kitchen with custom cabinets and stainless steel appliances. *Wow, this bitch must be loaded*, Sandra thought to herself as she walked George into one of the bathrooms.

Alicia had her gun pointed at Sofie and sat her down in a chair at the dining room table which overlooked the golf course.

"Why have you turned on me, Sofie?" Tim asked. "You know those are all lies. You have to know. What's going on? How much did they pay you?"

"Tim, you've always been a fool. You think small. You're living in a Caribbean paradise, but you live like a commoner. I've repeatedly showed you the way to live like a king, and you rejected me at every turn. We could have been something."

"I have a family, Sofie. I've told you I would never leave them."

"Get to it," Alicia Blake said. "We don't have time for this. Who's setting us up? Who gave the order for the 'shoot first'?" Alicia demanded, punching Sofie in the mouth.

"Stop it," Tim demanded as he pulled Alicia away from her. Sofie smiled, blood covering her teeth.

"That bitch is as guilty as the rest of them," Alicia said.

"Wait a second," Tim said, "Let me get you something for that." Tim headed for the kitchen to get a rag for Sofie's busted mouth. A single shot rang out, bullet to the head. Sofie fell out the chair. As Tim returned to the room, all he could see was Alicia Blake standing over her.

"What have you done?" he was saying as Alicia threw herself at him and knocked him to the ground.

"It wasn't me. Came from the window. We gotta go. Stay here." Alicia crawled toward the bathroom where George and Sandra were, but they were on their way to them. "Check wherever you can—bedrooms, closets. Find something. We gotta get some leverage. Move, people. Get to her garage, you three." She tossed some keys laying on a table to her sister.

"We'll take the boat. Come with me, Muscles." She was now referring to George. "The rest of you, get her car, and get the fuck outta here."

Tim was looking at Sofie's lifeless body as the three of them made it to the attached garage. Alicia motioned for George to stay still. He'd seen this before from her and did not move. She peeked out the window overlooking the golf course and realized the bullet was meant for Sofie and not them. They didn't want her to talk. There were no more shots and no movement. She began searching in the main bedroom. She came across the briefcase with the money.

"Let's go," she said to George.

"What's in the case?" he asked. She just gave him a stern look, briefcase in one hand and gun in the other. She peeked outside and could see her sister, Tim, and Louis driving down the pathway toward the road. She and George were just about to get into the boat when she felt a gun upside her head and a voice ordering her to drop the gun. George got in the boat being held at gunpoint. The boat still had the shuttle scraps and all the materials and evidence they had gathered thus far.

The sky was getting dark. The cloud cover was moving out toward the sea, right where Tim had thought it would, over toward Palm Island. There would be hundreds of tourists there, getting ready to take the boats back to the mainland from the private island, one of Aruba's premiere excursions. Palm Island had it all—banana boat rides, a zip line, beaches, snorkel tours, snuba, a waterpark, massages, an underwater helmet walk, and a nimbostratus cloud headed right for them.

CHAPTER 77

"What happened back there?" Sanchez asked as he, Natasha, and Caleb got into the boat. "That bitch just took one to the head. No doubt one of Creed's goons."

Alicia snapped back, "Look, we're on your side. We aren't terrorists, we're trying to end all this, but I have somewhere I've got to be, so shoot me now or let us go."

"She's telling you the truth," George said. "Look up, that cloud is headed for that island. You have to get anyone that might be there to safety."

"That's Palm Island," Caleb said. "There's got to be hundreds, if not thousands of people there."

*   *   *

The sky's pool-like cloud was fast moving and almost upon the tourists on Palm Island. People on the island could see the monstrous cloud with what looked like blue and green flashing lights headed right for them. Some of the folks were busy doing other things and did not notice.

*   *   *

Sanchez was headed that way. "Natasha, call ahead to the island. Have them get everyone to some sort of shelter."

Sanchez, who had let his guard down, was yelling over the waves and sound of the engine. Alicia had spotted another tourist boat, not far from them. It was the *Jolly Pirate*, another favorite tourist attraction. They were anchored, and the crew and tourists were partying it up. There was music blasting and people drinking and swinging from a rope. They were not in the cloud's pathway. She could see they were towing a rubber boat behind them. Alicia pulled a knife out of her belt and put it right at Sanchez's groin.

"I'm sorry about this, but we have an exciting appointment we can't miss. We're going to take this cutter and head back. You three get to that tour boat and try and help get the people off that island."

She grabbed three life vests that were tied up to the side of the cutter, took Sanchez's and Caleb's weapons and phones, and made the three of them jump. Then she got a plastic bag, put their weapons and phones in it, and threw it in the water after them, but not before putting George's phone number in it.

"Call this number tonight!" she yelled as she pointed the cutter in the other direction and sped off.

George was smiling and shaking his head. "You just keep amazing me, little woman. Glad I'm on your side."

*   *   *

Screams were coming from Palm Island. At first, it was a just drizzle. With no shelter by the beach, some of the people sunbathing were the first to feel the pain from the rain. The drizzle quickly turned into showers, and the beach became a bloody, horrific scene. One woman's guts were being devoured as she lay in a lounge chair. In the water, you could see the blood splashing onto the beach from the waves. It was terrible. Children and their parents didn't have a chance.

Elsewhere on Palm Island, things were not so much better. Natasha had called the warning in, and the *Jolly Pirate* was headed that way before they had to stop for fear of getting caught in the rain themselves. There was a food court in the center of the island, and many of the patrons managed to get inside without serious injury, but as the rain picked up, the death toll was growing. The water slide pool had turned into a pool of blood, bones, and mutilated flesh as people sliding down were exposed. The people inside could only watch in horror as those caught outside were being eaten alive until there was just blood and bones where they stood.

The screaming was terrible. People were pulling their own flesh off, trying to get the parasites off them. Some sacrificed their lives, trying to help their loved ones. The rain poured down on the island for about a half hour. There was death everywhere. Maybe a hundred people scattered about the island survived.

Sanchez, Caleb, and Natasha, along with the tourists on the *Jolly Pirate*, could do nothing as they stayed a couple of miles out from the cloud. After the rainfall stopped, the cloud just moved away. The sky was clearing above Palm Island.

*   *   *

Alicia and George landed at Eagle Beach, which was full of tourists. They pulled up to a pier restaurant, unloaded the boat, and were able to get hold of a taxi driver whom they hoped didn't recognize them. They headed for the Caribbean Palms Villa, where his family was waiting.

CHAPTER 78

Creed and Damon were in the governor's office, Creed with a cigar in mouth and drink in hand.

"Sofie's dead. They killed her," Creed was explaining to the governor. "You have to get your people to cooperate in this search. We're coming up empty, and the few times we've had them in our sights, they got away."

"Why would they kill Sofie?" the governor asked.

"Well, I had my men check her home. They apparently robbed her desperate for cash. Do you know what she did with her portion of the payout?"

"No," the governor answered. "And you are never to speak about that to anyone. This is what I know: people are still dying on my island, under my watch, and you're sitting here in my office. I've given you all the resources you asked for, and what have I got?"

Creed got up from his seat, looked over at Damon, walked over to the governor, blew cigar smoke in his face, slapped him, pulled out his gun, and pressed it to his head.

"Look here, Mr. Governor. I don't give a shit about your two-bit gold digger bitch." He put the gun against his windpipe and then under his throat. "I will blow your fucking head off, burn down this building, and go fuck your wife and daughter, and have Damon fuck your son. Do we understand each other?

"Someone is helping them. Someone we're overlooking. Get me the list of Tim Coles's family and friends, everything. He's the key," Creed said, putting his gun up and patting the governor on the top of his head. "Get your people to tighten up the search. Now!"

"Yes," the governor squeaked out, trembling. "I'm on it."

CHAPTER 79

Lethia Warfield, her daughter-in-law Sugar, and her grandchildren Lou Jr. and Brie were all out in the pool area. The kids were in the pool when her son Louis, Sandra, and Tim got back to the villa.

"Where's George?" his wife asked.

"They're on their way. There was some trouble, but he's fine," Tim said. "Let's all get inside."

Ten, maybe fifteen minutes went by in silence. Tim was on the phone with Dimo. He had bad news to tell the family, but he decided to wait till they were all here. The door swung open. It was Alicia and George.

"What happened?" his wife asked. "You've been shot."

"It's just a flesh wound, but we don't have time for that now. Time to get you all out of here."

"OK, bro. During all the excitement, we got offtrack. Does your theory work?"

"Yes, it does. I'm going to start mixing it up now, but we're gonna need the rest of the things on the list I gave Alicia."

Alicia broke in. "You'll have it tonight, but we have to get going now if we plan to catch our ride."

"There's something else you all need to know. Dimo just informed me there was a bomb explosion in Miami at a hotel called the Faena. Miami officials are calling it terrorism. They're saying two women blew themselves up when they were confronted by the authorities there after getting a tip about them smuggling a large sum of money into the US. Sorry, Louis, it was your wife and daughter," Tim informed everyone.

"There was also a story about a suspect tied to you, Sandra, who was killed while breaking into your condo, the *Miami Herald* reported. Your friend that helped us, Sean."

Sandra grabbed at Louis's hand, but he just pulled away. His son sat down on the couch and put his head down. Everyone was just silent.

"OK, *wow*, don't act so surprised. We told her not to go," Alicia said.

Sandra pushed her. "Stop it. Do you have no feeling for anything or anyone?"

"No, all of you, stop it," Louis said. "We have a job to do. Let's do it and stop Creed in the process. Too many people have died, and we have to finish this now. My theory works, so let's make it work and make those responsible pay. Tim, get to that lighthouse and start tracking those clouds. Get us the help we're going to need. Alicia, get the rest of our family off this island. We have one shot at this. Get going now."

He picked up his gear and headed for the empty bedroom. Sandra followed, and his son after her.

"Let's go," Alicia said, walking toward the door. George, Lethia, Sugar, and Brie went with her.

The sun was about to set when they arrived in Downtown Oranjestad, where the submarine was docked. The family was sitting nearby. Alicia made her way to the dock and was watching as all the employees made their way out of the building where operations and booking were set up, including the captain. She followed him as he said his goodbyes to everyone. Alicia was stunning, beautiful to the eyes yet very cunning. She made sure the captain saw her as she dropped her keys while approaching him. She picked them up and purposely dropped them again.

"Let me help you with that," the captain said as he bent down and picked up her keys, only to stand up to a gun being shoved in his gut.

"Turn around and slowly walk back to the building," Alicia demanded. She waved for the rest of the group to come to her.

"What is she doing?" Sugar asked her husband.

"Not quite sure, but let's just hope it works."

Alicia forced the captain to let them all in. "Get your maps," she demanded. "Don't ask questions. I don't want to hurt you, but we need a ride on your submarine."

Lethia and the rest of the family looked baffled. George was looking at a brochure about the sub, and he understood her crazy plan now. He looked at Alicia. "This better work."

Once aboard the submarine, Alicia, gun to the captain's head, told him where she wanted him to take them. The captain refused, and she hit him with just enough force on the back of the head to let him know she was serious. She also pulled out a picture of his wife and children. "Do you love them? Do you want to see them again?"

Then she whispered in his ear, "Captain, I won't hurt you, but someone will hurt them if you don't do exactly as I tell you. Take us down 60.96 meters, that's 200 feet. We should be able to avert radar there."

Everyone was sitting looking at the darkness of the sea. It was very quiet, very scary.

"Miss, this submarine is only certified for dives of 40 meters or 130 feet."

"Do it," she demanded. "And no sonar. Use the voyage management system. You have the destination chart."

Alicia was confident her plan would work. She had staked out claims in these waters before. There were sunken ships in the area, but it should not be a problem to navigate around them. They just had to stay undetected by the Dutch Caribbean Coast Guard from Aruba, and the Bolivarian Navy of Venezuela—at least she thought so.

Alicia had contacted her friend to let him know all was going as planned on her side. He responded, saying all the materials she asked for and the safe house were ready. Transportation was waiting for the family to take them to the Dunes Hotel and Beach Resort on Margarita Island, and his men were ready to load up the submarine.

What Alicia had not planned on was being followed. They were being tracked by a large charted fishing boat named *Lady Smooth*.

CHAPTER 80

It was now ten o'clock. Sanchez, Caleb, and Natasha were at the Hard Rock Café bar watching the *News Now at Ten*. The weather report was still being distorted, and deaths on Palm Island had not been reported. Sofie's death was being called a robbery by the terrorists, and their pictures were being flashed during the broadcast. The reward had been doubled. Alicia had told Sanchez to call, but it wasn't time yet.

The carnival was dying down for the night, and Aruba's nightlife was gearing up again. What was strange about the weather report was that they didn't mention the cloud that now was a full white circle around the island and darkness in the middle. Everyone was looking up at the sky and had a theory on what it was or what it meant. There, however, were no blue and green flashes, and people just went on about their nighttime activities.

"What do you think it is, Natasha?" Caleb asked.

"What else could it be?" she answered while downing her third shot. *"Rain clouds of death.* That's what the people are calling the clouds now."

CHAPTER 81

Everything went just as Alicia had hoped it would. The family was headed for the safe house, and the submarine was now packed with all the materials Louis had asked for. Alicia, George, and the captain were on their way back to Aruba in the dark waters. They were unaware of the activity above them because radio waves did not travel well through conductors in saltwater. They were being hailed by the Dutch Caribbean Coast Guard, who suspected something was going on in the dark waters. The DCCG was just about to launch an underwater spy drone when their hail was answered by the fishing vessel *Lady Smooth*.

* * *

Smooth, as the Islanders called her, owned the vessel and was no stranger to the coast guard. She was the number one sought-after fishing charter on the island. She and her three daughters originally from Michigan had moved to the island about fifteen years ago and set up shop. All four were beautiful, fun, easygoing women with a talent for marketing, sailing, catching, and cooking the fish at the restaurant they owned. The coast guard shined the lights on her vessel and asked her why she was out so far. Smooth explained that she and her daughters were dropping crab pots for the morning. One of the daughters appeared from the water and climbed aboard the ship as the coast guard continued to shine their light on her vessel.

Smooth explained that the netting had gotten tangled, and her daughter had just unhooked it. The captain of the DCCG told her she was out too far and had set off a sonar surface buoy designed to catch smugglers. She needed to move inward, back toward Aruba territory. Smooth apologized for the mishap and thanked him. Dinner for him and his crew would be on her the next time they visited her restaurant.

The captain, distracted by Smooth's daughter pulling off her scuba gear, gave the all-clear signal, and the guard turned their ship around. Smooth headed back to Aruba shores at full speed in an attempt to catch the submarine before it docked and Alicia got away. Smooth made it back to the dock first and secured her boat, her and her daughters fully armed. With her key to the *Atlantis* building, she entered and waited.

Ten miles out from the docking area, Alicia had gotten the call from Captain Sanchez. She instructed him to bring a truck to the docking area to unload her cargo. Sanchez reluctantly agreed. After the submarine captain secured the sub, Alicia ordered him back into the building. While waiting for Sanchez, the three of them were surprised by Smooth at gunpoint.

"Don't move, drop you weapons," the voice of a woman said.

Alicia, without hesitation, quickly turned her gun on Smooth and replied, "No, honey. I think you better drop yours."

"Move aside, Ruben," Smooth said to the captain.

George had been standing next to Alicia, wondering if she was about to shoot this beautiful woman, when three other women emerged, guns pointed at him and Alicia.

"Drop your weapon now. I won't tell you again," Smooth demanded. "Dead or alive, the reward says. It's up to you."

With all her experience, Alicia knew she was outnumbered and had no choice. She lowered her weapon.

"Look, you don't know what you're doing. Let me explain," George said as he was pushed against the wall by one of the daughters.

Smooth asked the captain if he was OK, and he said yes.

"Watch them. Tie them up," she told her daughters.

"Look, lady, whoever you are, you're making a big mistake," Alicia said.

"My only mistake is not dropping you where you stand now. Shut up and get over there before I do."

At that moment, Sanchez and Caleb burst into the door, guns drawn.

"Hold it, Smooth. Don't do it!" Sanchez shouted. "Everyone stand down."

The girls pointed their weapons at Sanchez and Caleb, Natasha was behind them, filming the whole ordeal.

"What is this?" Smooth demanded to know. "You're protecting these terrorists now? After what they have done? She killed Najee and Sheila, you said it yourself."

"Just hold on, Smooth, ladies, let me try and explain," Sanchez ordered. "But first, holster your weapons. No one needs to get hurt here."

"Explain what I saw then. I saw them kidnap Ruben. I followed them on my boat. They obviously went to Venezuela, I wanted to see her up close one more time. She is responsible for my best friend's death, and it would have been me and my girls had I not turned down their offer to charter my boat that day."

"What is she talking about, Alicia?" George asked.

"Don't know for sure, but we don't have time for this right now. Sanchez, we need to get the cargo on the truck and get out of here now before you-know-who comes a calling."

"She's right!" Caleb got in the conversation, looking at Sanchez.

"OK, Smooth, you have to trust me on this. They can explain it to you, but now we could use your help, and we don't have time to stand here and debate about it. Walk away now, or come with us. Help us and hear them out. That goes for you too, Captain Ruben." The group unloaded and then loaded the cargo from the submarine to the truck that Sanchez, Caleb, and Natasha had brought. Smooth had two of her daughters stay behind and return to her boat, one with her. The group left the docks and headed back to the villa.

CHAPTER 82

Tim was in the radar tower next to the lighthouse. He'd gotten Dimo to help him rig some equipment to better help him track the clouds. He had been watching the ring-shaped cloud that just seemed to hover without any movement. He was researching on O-shaped clouds, which were common, but this one he knew was not. This created another problem. If the blue and green lights showed up, then this meant nothing could get to the island, and nothing could get out. It seemed as if the cloud was trying to push everything to the center. NASA had satellite images of formations like this, but the website had suddenly been shut down and told users to try later. Not surprising, he thought to himself.

He made a couple of calls asking those he knew he could trust to come to church tomorrow at the Alto Vista Chapel.

* * *

Lou Jr. was fast asleep in a bedroom down the hall. Louis and Sandra had done all they could with the materials they had and even tested the arm again using different methods of dispersing the mixture. But now it was quiet. It was around 1:00 a.m. They waited, sitting out by the pool and looking at the cloud formation.

She asked, "Do you think we have a chance of surviving this?"

"There's always a chance," Louis said as he moved toward the pool, sat down, and put his feet in the water.

"I'll be right back," Sandra said. "Got to pee."

She came back with a bottle of already mixed margaritas, two cups, a joint, and two towels, one wrapped around her. She sat down next to Louis, put her feet in the water, lit the joint, inhaled, wiggled a little bit, blew the smoke in his face, and turned up the bottle to take a hefty swig. She removed the towel, exposing her tanned golden skin, her voluptuous breasts, and her slender backside. She passed him the joint and slid into the warm pool. She swam halfway across the pool as Louis watched her well-rounded buttocks. He hit the joint and poured his and her drink.

She stopped in the middle and turned around, pulling her hair back from her face. She wiped her eyes as she slowly let the pool water drip from her lips. "Come on in, it feels nice."

Louis removed his shirt, and then his shorts and undies in one swipe. He turned the bottle up, taking a hefty swig, and then sat it down and disappeared underwater. He swam toward her underwater. He could see her backing away, coming to a stop as she came against the pool edge. He met her between her thighs at her spot and, with swift technique, began to blow and kiss her there. He came up for air, and before she could say or do anything, her legs had been put over his shoulders. He was back under, blowing and kissing, his tongue working its magic until he couldn't hold his breath anymore. Then he stood up and entered her slowly as she wrapped her legs around him. He pulled her to the middle of the pool, powerfully holding her firmly on him. They moved together passionately around the pool, not letting go of each other.

He pulled her to the edge where they had started. He held and stroked her as she picked up the joint and lit it again. He puffed it again, all while attending to her. Then he slid out. He sat on the edge of the pool while she came between his legs. She grabbed his manhood and thought of how pretty and hung he was. She opened wide and put it in her mouth. Louis downed his drink; he hadn't felt this feeling in forever. They moved all around the pool, all positions. He had her against the pool edge from the back. When he finally let go just about where they had started, he gently pulled out of her. Sandra turned around and kissed him. Then she grabbed a towel and looked around. It was still quiet, only the two of them, no one on any of the balconies or porches.

"Get dressed," she said, kissing him, "before someone comes." They both dressed up.

Back in the villa, when the door opened, there was a big fuss going on. Sandra was standing behind the bar, gun in hand, when George, Alicia, two women she didn't know, Sanchez, Caleb, another woman whom she thought she had seen somewhere, Natasha, and Captain Ruben all entered.

Caleb was just about to shut the door, and someone stopped it from closing. Simultaneously, guns pointed at the door from Sanchez, Caleb, Alicia, Sandra, Smooth, and her daughter. George had stepped out of the way. Louis stood by Sandra.

"My god," Tim said as he entered. "A little shaky, aren't we?"

"Tim, what's going on here?" Smooth asked. "Why are you with these people?"

Alicia broke in. "You know these crazy women?"

In a loud outburst, Smooth blurted out, "Crazy women?" Her gun was now pointed at Alicia, who also was pointing her gun back at her. Smooth's daughter had noticed that she had a twin and had Sandra in her sight.

"*Bitch, I will lay you down where you stand! This bitch killed my best friend!*"

"Calm down and stand down, everyone!" Sanchez shouted.

"Tim, you've got a lot of explaining to do."

"Excuse me, everyone, ladies," Louis said, hands in the air in a friendly gesture. "Did you get the materials, Alicia?"

"Yeah, we got 'em. Your family's safe, everything was going fine until whoever these two minus two showed up."

"Going well? You must really be out of your mind," Smooth said. "I watched your dumb ass kidnap Ruben, and then I tracked you to the border on my boat. I waited and saved your asses from the coast guard."

Smooth put her weapon in her back and stepped toward Alicia. Alicia holstered her weapon and stepped toward Smooth. "You want some? I've got plenty to give, whoever you are."

George grabbed Alicia and pulled her back.

"Hold on, Smooth, everyone. Please sit down. Pour some drinks. We're all in this together now, and it's going to take all of us to stop it. The clouds are changing. A big *nimbostratus storm cloud* is here and more on its way It's going to get here for sure while the carnival is in full swing," Tim said, downing his drink.

CHAPTER 83

It was six o'clock on a Sunday morning when Damon knocked on Creed's bedroom door. "Got a tip I think we should look into."

Creed looked over at the naked working girl he had reserved for the night. He shook her to wake her. "Get up and get out," he told her as he put his pants on. "Pay her," he told Damon.

She walked by Damon still naked. He gave her a $100 bill as she picked up her shirt and shorts.

"What's up?" Creed said to him.

"Someone said Tim and the twins were going to be at the Alto Vista Chapel this morning. We could get them after the service."

The door shut, and the girl seemingly was gone, but she was still standing right outside the door, listening.

"Call up some men from the quarantine roadblocks, have them meet us there at—what time does service end?"

"Ten," Damon said. "How many men?"

"Ten should be enough." Creed told him.

"One more thing, boss. Got a report saying it might be possible that some people are hiding out in one of the caves over on the north side. It could be the rest of them."

Creed told him to send ten men over to the cave to check it out. "We're going to the chapel."

Cheap bastard, the working girl thought to herself as she dialed a number on her phone. "They're coming to the chapel," she said and hung up.

*   *   *

It was customary for the governor and the ministers to all take part in today's activities in the parade. The governor knew he was in over his head, especially without Sofie. He'd made plans to take a short vacation after his duties were complete today. One more speech, one more day. His ship was sinking. He needed to get his family off the island. Too many deaths. He had let his greed get the best of him. But not anymore. He was going to call the director of NASA himself. In fact, he'd dialed the number and hung up before being put through. After the parade, he'd told himself.

*   *   *

Tim told his story on how he'd become involved with the family and twins. How they'd come to the station asking questions about their wild encounter flying into the clouds on the plane when they were just arriving. He recalled his conversation with the air traffic controller about the nimbostratus cloud. He also gave his account of how he'd gotten his friend Jason Pitts involved and how Jason paid with his life.

Louis went next, talking of how his mother had befriended Sandra at the café. She'd told them about how Captain Sanchez then believed Alicia might be responsible for the deaths on the fishing boat.

"No one is in the clear yet," Sanchez broke in.

"We came here to try and save our marriage, and now I'm told my wife and daughter are dead."

"Told that bitch not to go," Alicia mumbled to herself.

Sandra told everyone how, being twins, they would get these uncanny, unexplained feelings and emotions. "That's what brought me here. It was overwhelming. Then Sanchez and Caleb showed up at my resort. Alicia was in terrible shape. One thing is for sure, this is all related to the shuttle, which surely brought the parasites with it. I'll go on record saying this. NASA is to blame, and they will do anything to cover it up."

"Look here, everyone, lady, whoever you are. I lost five of my friends who were just trying to enjoy themselves. I had no idea about the rest of this shit, and I never meant for any of this to happen. Right now, Creed's on our ass, and what's done is done, but we have a chance to end it and make those who are really responsible pay," Alicia said, staring down Smooth and her daughter. "So either you're here to help, or you're not, and if not, get the hell outta our way."

"All this seems so unreal, so unpleasantly circumstantial. While I've seen the devastation with my own eyes and will be the first to admit that Creed, the governor, and the United States are trying to cover up something, we don't have proof."

"We do have the proof, captain," Louis said.

Sanchez continued, "I've been suspended, Caleb almost killed, and I have had friends and fellow officers killed. I'm here in a room with all of you who are being called terrorists. Let's finish this. Smooth, we're going to need you and your daughters on this one. Can we count on you?"

Sanchez looked over at Smooth and her daughter. Louis, George, Sandra, and Alicia were all wondering who this woman was.

There was a loud knock on the door. Everyone in the room froze, weapons drawn. Did they leave their guard down? A sleepy-eyed Lou Jr. came from the back, rubbing his eyes and stretching.

"Dad, I ordered a pizza, is that OK?" he asked, not shaken by all the guns pointed at the front door.

"Sure, son." Louis went to the door, Caleb right behind him. He slowly cracked the door open and stuck out a twenty. "Just sit it down on the ground."

"OK," the pizza guy said, "but that's not enough."

Louis pulled out twenty more. "Keep the change."

Alicia was at the window, looking around. The pizza guy sat the pizza down as asked and left. "Not smart," Smooth said. "You said you have proof. Show me. If I believe you, we'll help. If not, whoever is responsible for my friend's death will pay—" she looked at Alicia "—dearly."

"Then everyone come with me, so you all can see what we're up against," Louis said, heading toward one of the back rooms. Alicia had switched the money into a backpack while on the submarine and was noticeably safeguarding whatever was in it.

CHAPTER 84

The carnival was underway. There was a mixture of sun and clouds, the darkening O-shaped nimbostratus clouds visible throughout the island. The blue and green lights were flashing from deep within. It was a spectacular sight, but it was also creepy and frightening. Some parade goers opted to forgo, giving in to the rumors that the C.M.W.W. terrorists would strike today because of the size of the expected crowds, even though the governor was still insisting that everything was under control. At any rate, with a population of almost 105,000 plus tourists, the death toll would be catastrophic.

* * *

The Alto Vista Chapel was packed. After seeing the proof Louis offered, Smooth had called upon all her people to be present at the chapel this morning, including her other two daughters. This brought at least a hundred with another fifty or so on standby in the northern desert on horseback and dune buggies, all awaiting instructions. It also answered the question of who this woman was. Smooth was just about the most powerful, well-liked, respected woman on the island. She had come from a strong union background in the States, where she was one of the top organizers at a parts supplier plant for an automotive union. After setting up shop here in Aruba, she began to organize the private excursion vendors, hotel and casino workers, time-share recruiters, and many others, including the ladies of the night. She was well aware of the corruption taking place and had fought a courageous, furious fight with the hotels, casinos, western restaurants, and ministers after refusing to pay to play.

They had their own security set up outside the chapel, screening who was allowed in this morning service. Smooth had been quietly following the ongoing events since the day her friends Najee and Sheila got killed.

*   *   *

It was standing room only. Creed, Damon, and the men he'd ordered to report this turnout set up a perimeter spreading about a mile long and a half mile wide outside the chapel grounds. The men he ordered to the cave were awaiting his orders to go in.

*   *   *

It was time to face the islanders for Tim, Louis, Alicia, Sandra, Little George, and even Lou Jr. They all knew Tim, though he was first assumed dead, and now a wanted terrorist. The Americans they didn't know, but even they knew there was something shady about a group of Afro-American terrorists working with Venezuela to attack the island. Many of the people here knew someone, even tourists, who had been injured by whatever was coming out of the clouds. They also knew the governor, the now-murdered Sofie, and Creed were full of it, but they took the hush money payoffs anyway. But just by looking up at the strange clouds, they wanted more than just talk. They wanted something done. They wanted their peaceful "One Happy Island" back.

With the help of Tim, Captain Sanchez, Lieutenant Caleb, Natasha Stevie, Captain Ruben, and most of all, Smooth, with her three lovely daughters, the locals agreed to pitch in with Louis's plan to try and stop the imminent danger facing everyone on the island.

Tim was in constant contact with Dimo, who was in the lighthouse tracking the cloud precipitation while he was monitoring a Kestrel Meter (a handheld wind and weather tracker). Tim whispered into

Louis's ear, "We only have two to three hours, and then all hell's going to break loose. A severe storm is building up in the clouds."

In an attempt to keep ahead of Creed and his fifty or more men, Louis had Sandra type out instructions. This, along with new untraceable phones and walkie-talkies, were given out to members of the group to then instruct everyone of their jobs of controlling and detouring the crowds on land and the beaches. Others were tasked to go out to sea to attempt to dissipate the clouds and kill the parasites within them.

They had just about finished handing out everything when up to four loud booms were heard. All eyes looked to the sky, but then smoke started to spread throughout the crowd.

It was tear gas. Creed was making his move to disperse the crowd and draw Tim and the others out. He'd also given his men in the desert the order to move in on the cave. It quickly became chaotic at the chapel. Panic set in/ Creed's men were moving in, beating down the onlookers, all while asking, "Where are they? Where's Tim Coles? Where are the twins?"

The crowd started to trample over one another in a panicked attempt because of the effects of the gas, which caused a burning, watery sensation in the eyes, difficulty in breathing, chest pain, excessive saliva, and skin irritation. The extreme heat didn't help, it just elevated the effects more. Gunshots started to ring out. Over two dozen people were detained, with the rest barely getting out alive.

"Lock them in the vans," Creed ordered. "Let's go, they're headed into the desert."

The entire group managed to escape. They split up according to plan and headed toward there sites.

CHAPTER 85

Tim had contacted Dimo once more. Dimo was to get to the airport, which shouldn't be a problem. He was a top mechanic there. He was to shut down all airport computer systems, which meant no air traffic in or off the island. He was also to confiscate a helicopter and get it ready to be loaded with material to be brought to the airport, mainly a couple of rocket launchers.

Ruben was to get in touch with the coast guard and explain the situation in order for them to defer all ships and shut down the waterways surrounding the island.

Smooth and her daughters would coordinate with various sea excursion vendors. Fishing charter boats, with hers leading the way, were to be loaded with the modified rocket launchers that Louis, Sandra, and Alicia would make once they got back to the college they occupied earlier (in thirty minutes tops).

Jet Ski operators under Smooth would also be used to drag booms and skimmers out into the various beaches about 19 miles long. Then they would dump the mixed chemical solutions into the water under the projected locations of cloud movement. (The solutions were to be made up at the Palmera Rum Factory under Louis's supervision. Once he got there, so long as all hands were on deck, it would take 45 minutes, he'd estimated). This will trap the chemicals, like done for oil spills. They were hoping that the heat equator, which Aruba sat about twelve degrees north of, will evaporate the chemicals into the clouds, giving them a chance to spread with the help of Tim's projected wind gust from the normal trade winds that blew consistently. Sandra would head out to the desert with Tim. Caleb would lead the island's fire departments, who would add the solution to the fire engines or pumpers, which will enable them to spray down crowds that were going to get caught in the rain, minimizing the death toll to injuries.

Alicia was to then meet up with George. They were to have the locals change the parade routes toward the fire engines. Then they would head to the beach, where Alicia was going to dive and plant some heated underwater explosives just to make sure that the chemical solutions that poured into the sea would rise to the clouds. But she had a feeling her sister was going to need her. Creed was relentless and always had a backup plan. He would play trapped just to trap them.

Tim and Sandra, with about twenty people on horseback and dune buggies, headed to the northern desert. Along with those already waiting in the desert, their plan was to surround Creed, Damon, and the rest of his men. Creed had already fallen for their trap, believing some of them were in the caves. In fact, in the caves were more of Tim's neighbors from Saint Nicholas, armed and waiting. Most of the islanders recovered from the gas and set free those who were detained at the chapel. Smooth's people disarmed all the other men Creed had at the quarantined roads leading to the desert.

Sanchez and Natasha went to get the governor and force him to the news station, where he would publicly recant his lies. Everything was to be done simultaneously.

There was rumbling starting in the clouds. It was loud, but there was no rain yet. Creed's men had entered the cave. There was a fierce gun fight. The plan was not to kill his men, just disarm and detain them. Creed had given different orders: kill if necessary—a nice way of saying "shoot to kill." In his mind, he only needed Tim and Sandra alive since they were truly the only ones Jason Pitts had made contact with. This would allow him to recover the shuttle scraps and then kill them. Creed and Damon had followed some of the islanders posing as Tim into the desert. Once they caught up with them, he knew he'd been tricked, and just like in Custer's last stand, he, Damon, and the ten men with him were surrounded. Creed and his men quickly surrendered their weapons. Creed then lit a cigar.

"Bravo, Mr. Coles," he said, clapping. "How surprisingly brilliant of you." He turned around in a full circle to survey the situation. Tim, Sandra, and the others dismounted their horses and buggies.

"Do you really think it ends like this, Mr. Coles? Do you think you can just tell the world what really happened? Ms. Blake, of all people, you should know better. In fact, here's what I'll do. Give me the shuttle scraps and whatever other evidence you have, and we'll let you live. Even give you your old job back. Mr. Coles, you can come work for us too. Your names will be cleared, you'll be greatly compensated for foiling the Venezuelans' plan, and everyone goes home happy."

"Are you mad?" Sandra said. "You murdering bastard. It's over. This is where it ends."

Shots rang out from inside the Gold Mill, where Creed had another twenty men hiding. "Now drop your weapons," Creed demanded. "You had your chance."

Everyone did as ordered. Damon and the rest of the men picked up the weapons. "Line them all up, but these two," he said, referring to Tim and Sandra.

"Kill them." Gunfire rang out. Twenty men lay dead.

"You men, drag them into the mill. The rest of you, stay there," Damon said, referring to the men still in the mill

Creed walked up to Sandra and punched her in the stomach hard. She fell to the ground.

"Bitch, that's for having me chase your ass all around this *fucking island. Where are the scraps?*" he shouted as he kicked her in her side. Tim tried to move forward, but Damon hit him in the head with his pistol.

"Don't worry," he said. "We got something for you too."

Thunder rumbled. Creed pulled Sandra up by her hair. "Where, bitch?" he asked while slapping her in her mouth. He then nodded at Damon.

Damon said, "What about you?" He kicked Tim in the stomach. As Tim bent over, Damon hit him in the back of the head.

Then there was a loud explosion. A fireball erupted, and the Gold Mill collapsed, killing all of Creed's men inside. Next, a single shot rang out at Creed's feet as Alicia and George came from the sea, up from behind the rocks.

"That's right, *motherfuckers*! Drop the guns!"

"Watch that one," she told George, looking at Damon.

"You OK?" she asked her sister, helping her off the ground. "Did he hurt you?"

Sandra had a bloody lip and was holding her stomach. "I'm all right," she said, spitting on Creed.

"You going to shoot me, bitch? Just do it, get it over with," Creed said, dropping his cigar and stomping it out.

"Nah, motherfucker. Got something better planned for you. I'm about to whoop that ass. You three, watch his boy," she said to George, Tim, and Sandra.

"Sit down on the ground," George ordered Damon, who was about the same size as him.

"I'll get some rope," Tim said. He kicked Damon and went and got some rope from one of the horses, He tied Damon's hands behind his back. He looked at George and Sandra. "Is she for real?"

"Dead serious," George said.

The thunder came again. "We have to go," Tim said.

"Who?" Alicia said as she moved toward Creed. He sucker punched her in the mouth, and she fell.

"Bitches, please. Who do you think? The same person who hired your ass to find them ordered you dead." He moved in to kick her, but she grabbed his foot, and with a swift, sweeping kick to the back of his foot, he was on the ground.

"Get up, motherfucker. One more time, who's behind this cover-up?" Alicia did a roundhouse kick, this time catching Creed in the jaw. Damon had slipped his hand out of the ropes and was just about to make a move when George kicked him in the face.

"No, you don't. This is for my sister-in-law and niece, you punk-ass bitch." He then shot him in the side. Alicia elbowed Creed in the head, and he fell.

"Give me that rope!" she shouted. "If they move, shoot them."

She tied them together back-to-back by ankle and throat, their hands bound behind their backs.

"Give me that cigar." She lit the cigar and put it in Creed's mouth. She went to her backpack, opened a canister, and carefully got a parasite. She placed the parasite on Creed's cigar and then picked up her gun and pointed it at the two men.

"Do it!" Creed shouted, blood starting to run from his mouth.

"Not a chance," Alicia said as she took out her knife and stabbed Creed in the hip area. "You fellows enjoy the rain. And didn't anyone ever tell you, those things will kill you," she said, referring to his lit radioactive, parasitic cigar.

"Let's go," she said to the others as the thunder rumbled once more.

"No!" Damon was shouting. "You can't leave us here! What about the rain? No! Come back!" He kept yelling as he attempted to roll in the desert. Creed was unable to say anything as his throat had started to swell. The three of them got in separate dune buggies, slapped the horses to get them started, and headed for the other side of the island.

*   *   *

All the chemicals had been placed inside the skimmers and booms. The fire engines were loaded, the rocket launchers set. Sanchez had the governor make the announcement at the parade for everyone to take cover, but some still didn't listen. Then, at the station, he made an emergency broadcast. Alicia and the others had not been seen. Louis had set fire to the chemicals in the sea to compensate for Alicia not setting the explosives off underwater. The burning chemicals poured smoke into the clouds as the beaches and the Caribbean Sea looked like it was ablaze. In the sky, you could see the dead radioactive parasites falling from the clouds, the blue and green lights slowly fading. The waters were smoking once they hit it. It looked like a sea of dead maggots, millions of them.

Smooth had fired off the rocket launchers equipped with the special firework-like explosions filled with the solution just as the rain had started on another beach. With the same effect, the fire department was hosing down those who had decided to stay and risk their lives—mainly tourists who had no clue what was going on. All in all, there were still heavy injuries. Those who didn't follow the detours were badly mutilated, but the chemicals surely reduced the number of deaths to under a hundred out of five thousand estimated attendees.

Out of the millions of raindrops that fall out of the clouds, it's been estimated that raindrops falling from 6,500 feet at an average speed of about 14 miles per hour would hit the ground in just over 6 minutes. This gave the crowd a chance to get out from the rain and get inside nearby businesses during the start of the light rain.

*   *   *

The rain had completely stopped on the side of the high-rise hotels on Palm Beach. The hospitals were full again. The cleanup of the dead was at a minimum. On the north side of the island, the rain was pouring. It had taken longer for the winds to transport the chemicals. The rain was catching up to the three people trying to outrun it. There was a hovering sound above them and loud explosions. Smooth was firing the rocket launchers at the oncoming rain filled with the chemicals. Dimo sat the chopper down, and the three boarded. The chopper took off again, headed for the sunny part of the island.

Creed and Damon got the worst of it as they lay helpless in the desert, unable to untie themselves. Creed's face had been totally mutilated by the singe parasite, yet he was still alive. When the rain reached them, it was a pitter-patter of light but rapid taps of live radioactive space parasites.

*   *   *

Three weeks later, everyone met up at Smooth's restaurant. It had been a long first week after. Sanchez and Caleb were busy testifying about the indictments handed down on the governor and members of his cabinet, all while getting reinstated passports for Louis, Lou Jr., and George. The twins were in no hurry, so they kinda just caught up and patched things up between them. Louis had been out on Smooth's boat a couple of times with his son. He liked Sandra, but they both knew better and decided to stay in touch.

*   *   *

It was final now. They were all in the clear. The president of the United States fired his own hand-picked director of NASA, Luther Page. No charges would follow. Aruba's governor was going to sit in the jail in the back of the island for a long time. Tim had his family back with him and was taking an extended leave of absence. Natasha was promoted to station manager. They drank, ate, laughed, cried, and left.

*   *   *

When they got back in the States, the Alexanders held a hero's memorial for Big George. They also made sure everyone knew Louis's wife and daughter were innocent from the charges of terrorism.

Three months later, a package arrived in the mail for Louis, with cash in the amount of $250,000. The same thing showed up for his brother and mother.

One year later, Louis and son were back in Aruba. He'd promised his son he would go on the sea BOB. Things were quiet and normal. No one knew who they were. They were riding the underwater BOBs around the shipwreck when Lou Jr. started to see blue and green flashing lights coming from within the sunken ship. His dad was looking at the seafloor at what appeared to be dead fish carcasses. Then there came a light explosion. It was enough to knock Lou Jr. off the BOB and send Louis scrambling to reach his unconscious son. There was another diver in the water that helped him pull his son to safety on a rubber raft floating above. There was a fishing vessel nearby, and they headed that way.

Once aboard the boat, Louis gave his son mouth-to-mouth. He was going to be all right. He turned around. The woman took off her scuba mask. It was Alicia Blake! The fishing boat was *Lady Smooth*!

CHAPTER 1

THE BEGINNING!

First, I would like to thank my Lord and Savior Jesus Christ for all the blessings he has bestowed upon me.

A deep thanks to my family, and friends for the continuous support, patience and encouragement. Thanks to my new family Love you all. Thanks Nate and Rob Roach for helping me see my vision come to life. And special thanks to all my readers past and future. Enjoy!

86040349R00131

Made in the USA
Lexington, KY
07 April 2018